HIGH PRAISE FOR KIRK ALEX

Lustmord: Anatomy of a Serial Butcher

"Great book. Dark—yes. Grotesque—certainly. Sexually explicit—without a doubt. And the writing is excellent. Character & dialogue, is as real as it gets. A terrifying, non-putdownable horror."

—Jeff Bennington, K/Book Review

Zook

"**Zook** was a zoo ride! All of the characters were well written and you find yourself unable to put the book down! You might even find it a little sad. ***** out of 5 stars."

—NetGalley

"A very good book that will leave you on the edge of your seat. If you make it through the first 2 or 3 chapters, you will not want to put the book down. **** out of 5 stars."

—NetGalley

Ziggy Popper at Large:
14 Tales of General Degeneracy, of Mayhem & Debauchery – for the Morally Conflicted & Borderline Criminal

"Gruesome, violent, awesome! I absolutely LOOOVEEE Kirk Alex. I am always ready for his next book!! Extremely entertaining. A whole lot of violent, and just what I was looking for. Private detective Felix "Choo-Choo" Buschitsky and Ziggy Popper are now my two favorite characters. ***** out of 5 stars."

—NetGalley

nonentity
–A Rant For Those Who Can't–
Presented as a Novel

"This is a quick read and engrossing. I found myself wanting to know what happened. Many of the situations were funny in the way they were presented. Fast, easy read."

—NetGalley

The book takes us through the trial and trauma of looking for a new job, any kind of job—manual labor, delivery, warehouse man. Anything but driving a taxi, our character's previous employment back in the City of Los Angeles. He is sneered at, looked down upon and insulted in his search for a job—really a search for identity—and in the end he perseveres and lands one. A bakery gig.

"Author Kirk Alex loves Bukowski and Kerouac and it shows; his prose is swiftly moving and terse and dark and angry and ugly. There is no wiggle room in what he writes and what he sees; bad is bad and good is rare. Apparently the writer has struggled a long time to get this book published, and it's a good thing he did. This will grab you by the heart and choke the breath out of you—and by book's end, you'll thank him for doing it."

— Steven Rosen, Curled Up With A Good Book

"This is another well done, honest and heartfelt piece of writing from Kirk Alex. At one time or another, everyone can identify with Chance, being unemployed and very low on funds. It's short, easy to read, and well worth the reader's time."

—Paul Lappen, Dead Trees Review

Working the Hard Side of the Street — Selected Stories / Poems / Screams

". . . this is a nicely put together piece of work."

—BookLore

"City of Angels? Maybe for that couple of percent of people who get anywhere near that thing called 'fame and fortune.' Everyone else is just trying to get by in a place where, if you don't have the right job and a flashy car, the odds are very much stacked against you.

"This book is excellent. It's full of honest, heartfelt writing that certainly shows a very different view of Hollywood."

—Paul Lappen, Dead Trees Review

"**WORKING THE HARD SIDE OF THE STREET** — Selected Stories **/ Poems / Screams** is an anthology of powerful, caustic, original tales and poems by Kirk Alex about the ups, downs, and hard knocks of Hollywood's seamy underbelly. The perspective of a "fly- on-the-wall" cab driver provides a piercing realism and insight into the vicious clashes and personal struggles that lie hidden underneath the entertainment capital's glossy, photo-touched exterior. **WORKING THE HARD SIDE OF THE STREET** is recommended as a gut-wrenching read for both its candor and bravado."

—The Midwest Book Review

BLOOD, SWEAT and CHUMP CHANGE –
Taxi Tales & Vignettes

"After reading BLOOD, SWEAT AND CHUMP CHANGE — Taxi
Tales & Vignettes by Kirk Alex you understand why the American
Dream needs liposuction. It's all here: Hate, poetry, sadness, hope and the
ache of an aloneness that never goes away. Belly up!"
   —Dan Fante, author of Mooch & Spitting Off Tall Buildings

Fifty Shades of Tinsel
A Novel

"This story is a bit dark and to say there is a lot of sex is an understatement.
Jimmy's journey is an interesting one. **** out of five."
   —NetGalley

BY KIRK ALEX

Crime Fiction:
Throwback: Love, Lust & Murder – Book One
Backlash: Love, Lust & Murder – Book Two
Disturbed: Love, Lust & Murder – Book Three
Ziggy Popper at Large – 14 Tales of General Degeneracy, of Mayhem
& Debauchery – for the Morally Conflicted & Borderline Criminal

Horror:
Lustmord: Anatomy of a Serial Butcher
Zook

Erotic Romance:
Fifty Shades of Tinsel
(graphic carnal situations not meant for prudes)

Chance "Cash" Register Tucson Working Stiff Series:
Take This Job & Shove It!
Journey to the End of the Week
A Confederacy of Mooks
nonentity

LA Cab Exploits:

**Working the Hard Side of the Street — Selected
Stories/Poems/Screams**

Blood, Sweat & Chump Change — Taxi Tales & Vignettes

Eddie "Doc" Holiday Contemporary Mystery Series:

Hush-Hush – Holiday #1

Hubba-Hubba – Holiday #2

Hard Noir – Holiday #3

BACKLASH

Love, Lust & Murder

Book Two

KIRK ALEX

TUCUMCARI PRESS

TP

Tucson — 2018

ISBN: 978-0-939122-56-1 (6x9 pbk)
ISBN: 978-0-939122-57-8 (ePUB)

Dedicated to Sean Chercover for writing a couple of
private eye thriller masterpieces, namely
Trigger City & *Big City, Bad Blood.* Kudos.

Chapter 1

The stalking phase of the hunt was on. I worked my way back to the North Hollywood area. And I had a real partner with me this time, a mixed-breed pit bull stray I befriended along the way and named *Payback*. *Redd Dogg* is what I went by this time. Couple of mutts; that's what the current incarnation of this team was. And the trio? Well off now. Graham's life insurance policy had paid off a while back, big time. And Rinelle? Long dead. Murdered. By assailant and/or assailants unknown. Until the mook, Jamal, to avoid Death Row, confessed. He'd beaten her with a ball bat, chopped her up with a meat cleaver and fed parts of her to animals at a zoo. And he'd done the same to some other peeps. Swell fellow. He'd been the major motivator, the punk who'd initially pushed Rinelle (who pushed Margie) into pumping the antifreeze into Graham. How nice. Until he busted Margie's mother spiking his *Night Train* with same. Even sprinkling his corn flakes with roach killer.

"Hear what I'm sayin'? Boric acid. Claimed it was powdered sugar. Gimme nose bleeds and runnin' shits. Belly cramps." He lost it. "Took her ass out." His claim. What he said. According to media. "Good riddance to bad rubbish." His own words. "Ho was a Black Widow. Owed me big time."

Turned out to be true: Margie's demented mommy Rinelle had poisoned her first few hubs the same way she had buried Margie's step daddy Mario, by lacing their Gallo with antifreeze, at times resorting to other means. Nobody really knew what her final tally was. When Margie's stepfather—of *Rossi Bail Bonds*—kicked the bucket, the house had been paid off; no mortgage—until Rinelle decided to refinance and blew most of it on crack and meth that she got from Jamal and his pals; the rest on one-armed bandits wherever she could find them: Vegas, Nevada; Gardena, CA; Atlantic City.

Monica was the primary force behind a legit production company and was producing cable tv specials, documentaries and motion pictures. She did docs on Sam Adams, Harry Truman, Honest Abe. Quite successful. Worked with the biggest stars. Margie? The other half of this dynamic duo and co-owner of said showbiz enterprise? Acted in substantial productions; their own as well as those initiated by others. She never carried a film playing the main lead, although she did just fine playing second or third principles. Was also co-producer with Monica on some things, as well as screenwriter; living together in an exclusive part of Receda in the San Fernando Valley.

Now, anyone in the know will tell you: San Fernando is the main hub and center of the multi-billion dollar a year porn industry. It is also a known fact that more than a few major corporations have a hand or two in this money-making machine. And like so many on the mainstream and legit Hollywood side who got their start this way, put together their grubstake to make it in Hollywood in this fashion, by dabbling in smut, so did ambitious Monica and her enterprising honey. No, they didn't appear in these films; they were far sharper than that, in that they were catalysts behind their productions and owned them outright. This was the only way to go—if you intended to make bank. Of course this was how they had funded their maiden mainstream pet projects that got them in the door, that and some of that money the insurance company paid off. Furthermore, they continued to dabble in porn, using pseudonyms—as everyone in porn did, simply because it was not easy to walk away from easy money that smut was and continued to be.

Chambray? Long dead, one supposed. Her presence and memory traded in for a couple of cats, as Margie had never cared for dogs to begin with. Dogs had been Frank's thing. Monica had wanted to make her 'life-partner' happy and got her the felines.

Gay? Is that what they were? A couple? Sure. Stranger things have happened; and this turn of events was not what had bothered me at all. Far from it. Even Grozewski had divorced his wife, retired from the police department and moved in with some actor who played a detective on a tv series that Bruno was technical advisor on. Nothing unusual about any of it. Stranger things have happened in Tinseltown.

Chapter 2

Tailing them was not a problem. None of them knew what I looked like these days. The years in stir had left their mark. Hair had turned white. Face was lined and speckled with liver spots, what you could see of it, as I'd grown a full beard. Spots and wrinkles came with old age. Nothing to be done. My sight was not what it used to be and I was wearing eyeglasses now. Also, I drank a lot more. Mostly beer. Had to do with nerves. Life took its toll. You couldn't hide it, only fools denied it.

I got around in a used van, lived in it for the most part, took on what jobs I could find. Still suicidal, as always. I came to terms with this a long time ago. My fate. Damaged from the get-go, and certain things you just couldn't shake. Thoughts that my life amounted to nothing persisted. The way it was for most of us. I might've gotten somewhere early on, but hell, some handicaps were tough to overcome. But that didn't matter anymore. Rage fueled by a fucked-up beginning was no longer there, not an issue—that I could tell. Oh, the damage I certainly accepted at this point, but I was living with it. You had to, or else your skull exploded with the frustration and anger.

About the only thing that kept me going still was contemplating how to nail them, these cretins who wrecked my life to the point I no longer wished to go on. No ambition, no desire—for anything. I was no longer interested in driving for a living or pursuing stunt work. What a joke that was; the fact that I ever considered doing something like that for my bread and butter. I couldn't stand tv, movies and the assholes who made them.

4

In this respect, admittedly, I was not different from the late *mother-humper* himself: Frank Graham.

I didn't want to own a house or get married or have kids. None of it. Other than *payback*. Plain and simple. I was not a complicated man, after all. All I wanted was to see them pay the piper, and pay they would.

Meanwhile, there was tailing to be done, meticulous records of their every move recorded on video tape as well as in my notebook, comings and goings, who the friends were, where they ate breakfast, lunch, dinner, the clubbing and whose parties they liked being present at to be kept track of.

The biggest irony, I thought, the three were in the midst of turning the documentary about me into a feature film, with an actual narrative thread this time. So you knew right away, it was not a stretch, that they would fictionalize quite a bit of it. This irked me. The doc had been full of half-truths and outright lies and fabrications to begin with, now they were going to push the envelope even further in this area. Well, it was Hollywood. They did whatever the hell they felt like doing and called it *dramatic license.*

"When it comes to war, truth is the first casualty."

Who was it that said that? Not that it matters. But, yes; they were in the process of casting, and when they consulted their lawyer to see if they were legally obligated to get my permission, my consent, it was there that he informed them it would be wiser to change certain names, and that, also, I had been released.

Chapter 3

Did this bit of news make them nervous? Sure. Grozewski, more than the women, but they were apprehensive about it enough. There was no way to deny that I had been short-changed, mistreated; sent up the river for their gain. The spiteful bitches were concerned at last. And had hired a PI to look for me.

I took jobs that paid cash money, so there was no way to track me down. I didn't use credit cards, didn't have a phone of any sort. And my license? In another state, where I picked up the used ride, a van that resembled the one owned by Monica's son Modi: down to the same shade of tan and mag wheels. I added, to either door, the red lips and tongue hanging out, which was the Triple-Threat Divas/M&M logo.

Modi also had one of those idiotic *I heart LA* bumper stickers on his rear bumper. It pained me to do it, nearly made me vomit, but yes, I stuck one on there. Changing my license and registering the van at the Southern California DMV would only have alerted them, so I didn't go that route. I counted on accomplishing what was needed before I got pulled over by the rollers and aided this scheme along by getting around on a bicycle quite a bit, and by using public transportation the rest of the time.

I let my gray hair grow long, grew the beard; wore dark shades over the specs during the day and hats, all types of hats: wide brim, ball caps, that concealed quite a bit of my face. And what would I do for a gun? Weapons? I was willing to spend my own hard-earned cash on a few items, but thought to return to the park to see what I might dig up. Had no real idea that the late Graham's arsenal I'd buried years before would still be there or that I'd even be able to locate it.

Find the upper case 'G,' I reminded myself over and over. *Find the 'G.'* And take it from there.

It did require some doing. I showed at the park early one dawn and started probing and searching around, looking for the tree with the marker. And should I have failed to locate one or the other? So be it, was my attitude. I'd buy what I needed. Guns were not difficult to come by if you knew where to look. The average law-abiding citizen had a hard time, especially around these parts, but not peeps like me. Not that I gave serious thought to using a piece on them. A piece would have been too easy, too quick. I preferred something else; something more. I wanted these fucks to suffer. I wanted anything but a gat: claw hammer, screwdriver, ice pick, butcher knife, shovel, tire iron, cyanide, antifreeze, anything but a bullet that entered your vic's body and dropped them soon after.

So, I wanted suffering. I needed to see and watch them die. I wanted to make sure that they took a long time to expire, that it was painful and protracted, so that I could savor and enjoy every minute of it; hear the cries, pleas, begging. . . . I wanted maximum suffering. I wanted the bitches to taste fear and experience pain: psychological, emotional, physical. The gamut. Pain. Agony. Anguish. And I wanted that pig Grozewski to scream like the cunt that he was and beg and whimper for his life.

Extreme? By someone who rarely behaved this way? Yes, long before I got bagged and did the long stretch, I'd been in and out of the joint for this and that offense; theft, usually. As a kid even, I'd been far easier going, even with all that crap I'd been exposed to: mental abuse, beatings, starvation, but life warps you eventually, damages you eventually to the point your anger builds and escalates and ultimately boils over. Because it must. Because it has no other recourse.

And this is what was taking place here: a boiling over. Explosion.

Tsunami of hatred. I wanted to crush the trio for the vermin that they were; I wanted to dispatch and grind into the dirt all three because they were insignificant turds in my eyes, just as I had been insignificant to them years *before, during, and after.*

Want to *punish?* Feel like being *cruel?* Okay. *I can play this game. What's good for the goose. . . . The wrath of Fred Reed. . . .*

I located the tree, and dug up the tool box soon after. Opened it up. It was all there, wrapped in plastic as I'd left it: the pump action 12-gauge, several guns, and plenty of ammo for the works. I would clean and oil all of it thoroughly; get my hands on fresh ammo to play it safe. I would also pick up a few unrelated items: camcorders and sundry doodads: remotes and plenty of video tape.

Make a snuff flick? Was that the idea? Yes and no. The notion was to make a doc of the events as they unraveled in real time; a true doc. What a doc should be, as opposed to the one they had manufactured, by omitting facts and playing loose and free with motives. Most documentaries were like that: made by assholes with an agenda, trying to convince you to look at scenes and/or situations as they saw it, whether it was skewed bullshit or not. They rarely gave you the truth. Why? Why the need to manipulate? Because punks and pissants were warped in their take on things. Because the twisted punks and pissants were insecure and feared the truth and did not want you to be able to think for yourself. I say give it. Put it out there. To include every bit of detail in its gut-churning glory and let the gods decide who is right and who is wrong. Let the chips fall where they may.

Images, in this narrative, will be devoid of edits, slick or otherwise. Nothing ends up on the cutting room floor . . . but a body or two. Footage will be raw and real. Not unlike life itself.

Chapter 4

This is where I went after them, where the meticulous stalking commences. I got myself hired as dishwasher at *Pinocchio's Pasta*, one of their regular eateries in the Valley, and a couple of other places where they liked to get together and talk shop, plan productions, yack with actors and art directors and script writers and cinematographers and other porn and mainstream vermin of their ilk.

Things were going well, as far as I was concerned. I was in no hurry. It was fine, until late one night the *Pinocchio's Pasta* kitchen manager asked me to help the busser collect dirty dinner plates out there in the dining area. Problem was Monica and Margie and Grozewski and their pals were staying late, long after we had closed, drinking and yakking, and I was going to be busted, found out, if I went out. I had to come up with a reason why I couldn't do it, something legit.

Wearing dark shades over my eyeglasses at midnight was out. All I had to cover up with was my ball cap, which I pulled down low over my eyes, and kept my face turned away, plus the bifocals. Someone in their group called out to me; one of them, Grozewski, I think it was, or maybe his actor boyfriend, asking for another beer. I nodded my head, without turning. Returned to the kitchen with my tub full of plates, relaying to the manager their request.

"Go get it to them, then."

"But we're closed. They need to leave."

"They're regular customers. Generous tippers. We can't ask them to leave, and can't tell them they can't have their beer."

He ordered me to go in the walk-in cooler and get the beer. I hesitated, then finally went inside. Got the bottle of beer, and just stood there, sweating. What now? I was dead. If I went out there they were sure to recognize me. If I didn't, I got fired. I didn't care for the job, but felt I needed to stick around a while longer. I was a man on a mission, not from god, but someone far more legit: someone who'd been slighted, backstabbed and discarded. Nothing short of slaughter would do; my kind of slaughter. If I left the job on my own, I'd still be good, still be able to follow through on my plan.

I stepped out of the walk-in, slowly. Let the door close shut behind me. I could feel the manager's eyes on me. He knew I didn't want to go out there, but what he did not know was why. Still, he offered to take it. I said I'd handle it.

I picked up my tub, propped it on my shoulder before I stepped through the swinging aluminum door, and walked over to the table, making sure the plastic tub kept my face blocked and concealed from sight the entire time.

I paused at the table, placed the beer in front of Grozewski's boyfriend, who said thank you. I kept walking, collecting the other plates at the other tables.

When I returned to the kitchen, the manager gave me the look.

"Now, was that so hard?"

I shook my head. Didn't say word. I could have twisted his mellon right off. I had to stay calm, collected. To use an old, very old cliche: I had bigger fish to fry.

Chapter 5

With all the beer they were drinking it was just a matter of time for the twats to have a need to use the john. What I hadn't counted on was both going at the same time. Yes. To the 'powder room,' as the ladies like to say in classic Hollywood flicks.

What now?

I watched them go. Kept my eye on the door. I risked too much if I went in there with the two of them. Had to wait and hope that one came out alone. It didn't happen. Finally they emerged, and it was my loss. Until next time. Eventually one would go in there by herself. Either Margie or Monica, by herself, was fine.

At last it happened: Monica. Grabbed her purse. Hurried to the back where the restrooms were. Went in. I gave myself a reason to go in the back area and the short corridor where the water fountain was and johns were located, and slipped inside the women's crapper.

She was in the stall, talking on her cell phone. I looked about for where her purse might be. On the floor in the stall with her? And it very well might've been if the floor hadn't been littered with balled tissue, cigarette butts and general debris. She'd had no choice but to leave it on the vanity counter along the wall to my left.

First thought was to turn out the lights and take the keys, all of them: house and car, instead of making impressions with the clay kit I'd brought with, which had been the original plan.

I had to nix the idea soon enough. Missing car keys would've created the type of situation I didn't want when it came time for them to leave. So that was out. And should she have noticed that her house keys were gone? Too bad. It was the sort of chance I was willing to risk. Like most peeps, she was sure to have a spare set or two back at her and Margie's cribby. Besides, the fact her significant other would have hers with solved the issue. Tough shit if it didn't.

Now or never, I thought. Before actually turning out the lights, I played with the switch on the wall a few times, flicking it rapidly, to make it appear like an aftershock was about to cause an outage, then left them off. It was plenty dark. What light her cell gave off was a minor concern. The door to her stall was closed and it had to be good enough for what I needed to do. I was at the purse. Stuck my penlight in there.

"What the hell?" Monica was clearly buzzed on wine. "No, the light just went out. I should be used to these things by now. You would think." Then she said something else. I heard her laugh. "At a time like this, too. Would you believe it? I'm in the bathroom. Yes."

I found the house keys. Damn near went for the car keys, too. That's when I spotted what appeared to be a gun butt. I shoved a bankbook out of the way, and sure enough. It was a Glock. If I could have taken it without risking getting nailed, I would have. It was just as well, though. Now I knew the bitch was armed. Maybe even that other one had a piece somewhere. Why not? Had every reason: the guy they sent up the river was out and they needed protection. Only their guns wouldn't give them that. Too bad.

I left the purse, and was back at the light switch. Did the flicking number once again, as a reminder that the 'outage' had been a minor electrical issue after all, and left the lights on for good before easing out of the john. The manager saw me emerge from the corridor and gave me a dirty look. I wiped my mouth with the back of my hand. I figured my days were numbered.

A while later, while collecting dirty plates, I could hear Monica emerge from the back and walk to the table.

"That was weird. The light in the restroom went out. Thought we were experiencing another quake."

"Really?" Margie looked at her. "Light went out?"

"For a while. You guys never noticed?"

They shook their heads.

Chapter 6

Having access to the compound sure made it easier all around.
Wouldn't have to break any windowpanes now. Every little bit helped. I'd
be able to walk in through the front door, or maybe the rear. I'd drawn a
map of the house. Pretty much knew where everything was. I still didn't
have any way to open the gate, but that didn't matter. I'd be able to scale
the wall. Small price to pay. From there the place was mine.

Only I had to look out for other people. Her son lived in the Valley.
There was Grozewski and his bosom beau visiting on a regular basis; and
there was Margie and all those movie phonies she and Monica ran with.

So no, it would not be a cakewalk, but the keys sure made it a lot easier.

Chapter 7

The following night, at the restaurant, Margie, Monica and Grozewski were at it again, rating actors. I could hear them discussing certain Tinseltown mooks who might play me. Brad Pitt was one. Fuck Brad Pitt, I thought. He can't act.

"Kurt Russell."

Too effing old, I thought.

"Jack Nicholson."

No way. Old enough to be my father.

"Not for Freddie's part." Grozewski was talking. "To play me. Maybe Clint Eastwood to play Frank."

"Eastwood?" Margie hadn't cared for the idea from the sound of it. "That decrepit womanizing bastard should've been put out to pasture years ago."

Then the talk was on the female roles and the potential actresses versatile enough, with enough range to portray Margie and her wife Monica.

Some names were bandied about: Angelina Jolie, Laura Linney, Sandra Bullock. Dakota Fanning, and some others. I didn't keep up with Hollywood twats and didn't care. Not only was it pointless (because I would see to it that there would be no movie), but it made me sick to my stomach. Hollywood was a vastly overrated pile of dung—and here was the reason and proof. I knew whatever they did with it would be a lie.

"How about Charlie Bronson to play Frank?" I couldn't tell who made the suggestion. Frankly, at this point it made little difference.

"Part's not big enough. Besides, he dies early on, doesn't he? Like during the first third."

Fuck Charlie Bronson, too, I thought. Fuck all of them: *hoes* and *dogs*. Only the hoes and dogs couldn't stop yakking about it.

"Shouldn't Fred Reed be consulted with regards to some of this? At least offered some compensation?"

"Why? This is not about him. It's fiction at this point."

"The doc wasn't fiction."

"The doc was PD. Public Domain."

"True story."

"Everyone involved was compensated. He got sent up."

"He had it coming. He was a louse. Loser. Not worth bothering with."

Who was saying what I couldn't tell. I was not looking at them and went about collecting dirty plates and silverware. I thought of the different ways I could do the slime in: cyanide was one. I knew where to get it this time. It would have been so easy. A drop in each bowl of soup. They would've died on the spot. I wouldn't be able to get their bodies out of there and make them disappear; and I would've been bagged soon after. I didn't want that.

Chapter 8

I followed the two twats home that night. Even though I'd been there more than once before, thought it prudent to take another look, make certain I knew my way around, got to know the lay of the land better: not only the four-bedroom, five-bathroom Mediterranean style house they lived in, with guest house in back, swimming pool, gazebo, and the rest of it. I wanted to get to know what the neighbors were like a little better, their comings and goings; I needed to know about dogs and security, safest and easiest stretch of the wall to climb over, bind and gag the bitches, carry them out to the car and then drive through the wrought iron gate. These things required planning, not unlike breaking into a home and walking off with the silverware, cash, jewelry and other valuables. You wanted to slip in and slip out, without being detected.

Chambray, as noted, had been replaced by a couple of cats. Margie's choice. She hated dogs, and had pointed it out on more than one occasion years before. "*Dogs* are that *dawg* Frank's thing, not mine. I like cats."

I wore black, everything, down to socks, gloves, ski mask with perforations for eyes and mouth. Found myself in the patio area. Glass door that would have allowed access to the living room was not only closed, but definitely locked. No matter. I had a decent enough view through the curtains. Spied them sitting on the sofa, sipping wine and watching something on cable. Could've been one of their own productions, a doc or movie. Looked like a movie. Titles scrolled up.

Monica was the producer, director, co-writer. Margie had one of the female leads. Was also co-producer and co-writer. A couple of *triple threats*, as they like to say in Hollywood (whenever you had ability to do three different things and do them well enough to be recognized in the 'industry' for it).

I imagined even Grozewski was one of the 'triple threats' at this point: tech advisor, associate producer and *fluff girl*. Who knew? In porn, I had come to find out, that's what the chick who got the male lead's cock hard before the cameras rolled, flicked his knob with her tongue until he was stiff enough to get in there and do his job.

What Bruno was to me at this point, after all of it: *fluff twat*. It also came out, just as I had suspected, that he and Graham had had something deeper going than your casual *bro-mance*. No wonder Grozewski felt obligated to hound me the way he did. I had always suspected something of this nature, but hadn't been able to put my finger on it, and when it finally dawned on me, I refused to accept it. Why? Well, for one thing, Frank Graham had been one macho mother-humper, is why. Just like John Wayne. And yet, I'd always felt something peculiar about all that macho posturing. I liked the Duke, mind you, I just didn't care for the macho bullshit.

To me, true macho, the real macho men, never feel a need to carry that testosterone attitude on their shoulder. You knew you were a man inside and that was all that mattered. There was never any need to perch it on the shoulder and keep it there and constantly be reminding the world how tough you were, à la Dirty Harry, and some other phony Tinseltown mooks who went about it this way. Because, to me, usually, these fuckers were queer. Sucked pipe, and took bone up the crapper. Yep. Behind doors. This is the way it went. Tough guy on screen, pussy with a penis off-screen. It wasn't the fact they might be half gay that bothered me, it was the fakery, the phoniness; the three-dollar bill horseshit thing of it.

Chapter 9

Guess what? Fuck Duke Wayne and Magnum PI and Rambo, and the rest of those cocksuckers, because this thing with the twats was going where I expected it to: the wine glasses were lowered and the kissing started. Pecks, soft and tender, on the lips. Just the way women liked and were always bitching that the men they were with wouldn't take their time on when it came to smooching.

And it was tender and gradual, loving. And as much as I was taken by it, aroused by it, in fact, I loathed the cunts for it, for abandoning me in place of this. Dropping my cock and balls for vagina. How did that work? Why was it this way? How could any woman, especially these two, trade my dick for tits and muff? How was this possible? Was it always this way? Was lesbianism always this rampant and we just weren't aware of it? Am talking about through the ages: *Were bitches always after pussy, as opposed to dick?* And only had sex with us because it was expected and because it was the only way to get knocked up and have a kid? You hoped not. But you also wondered about it.

Margie picked up the remote and turned down the volume on the flick, and turned it up on the stereo system. Something slow and soothing rose up in volume. My groin was hard, and I didn't want it to be. I was not here to get rocks, not here for the sex. I was here on a mission, a mission I'd been contemplating for years, a do-or-die mission that I needed to carry out and then call it quits—forever. End my existence on this planet as I knew it.

So I needed to take my hand off my boner, and stay focused. Only the bitches wouldn't let me. They were at it, back to kissing lips and rubbing tits.

There was no denying who the boss was here. Margie. Margie, the one who'd been demeaned and dominated and mistreated and dissed by Frank Graham, was in total charge here. Go figure. Monica, on the other hand, the one who directed and very often called the shots out there, on set, was the compliant one who preferred to be dominated.

Did I get it? No. And I didn't give a shit, either. Because it was happening and I had no control over it and didn't want to have control over it. The only control I wanted was once I stepped into the scene and took charge and followed through on the payback I had in mind for the malicious she-devils.

Chapter 10

Margie remained seated on the sofa and maneuvered Monica so that she was kneeling before her, between her thighs. She guided her head down so that Monica would be planting kisses along the one inner thigh, then the other; then she had her move her head up, up toward her breasts, while Margie undid the buttons on her blouse. Monica's lips were kissing the cleavage, her lips moving to the right breast, then the top of the left. She had Monica pause long enough to undo the bra clasp in back. The bra was allowed to drop and tossed aside, and Monica was back on the full breasts, sucking in one of the nipples, then moving over to the other.

The way the sofa was positioned and the way the large living room with all its objets d'art from South America, Africa and the Middle East, had been designed, I had to do a bit of straining to the left to see exactly what was going on. The large flat screen tv was on a wall at the left side of the room, Margie and her wife with the capable tongue were on the right. Beyond the sofa was the large kitchen. The problem with where I was had to do with the sofa armrest, even with me standing, it was not easy to make out what exactly Monica was up to. Part of it, or rather, a great deal of it was blocked by Margie's left leg.

Margie had shoved her face down between her thighs. Pressed down with the palms of her hands on the back of Monica's head. Margie's own head was back against the backrest, tilted back, mouth open, grinning and sighing. Then it happened, she'd lifted her feet up and over Monica's shoulders, resting them there, and forced the other woman to go lower, pushing her face down against her nether region. This was a new one on me. Who woulda thunk? This was some wanton and raunchy behavior. Made my Jones go up. And stay up. I wanted to jump in; forget the bloodbath I had in store for them, and just fuck the shit out of both, then slaughter them like the worthless, useless backstabbers that they were.

Only I couldn't. I wouldn't. Because I knew there was no way they'd allow it. These two were certified lesbians at this point; and I was *persona non grata,* as any man would be. When women turned gay like this, if you were male you were out, period. *No ands ifs or buts.* They had no use for you or your penis. Besides, I needed to spare them both the shock of seeing me. Not for their sake, but more for mine. I couldn't afford the disruption and absolute chaos it would have resulted in.

Margie guided the other's mouth back up again. Kept her there. Margie was screaming, her body quivering. She was orgasming; a whole series of orgasms followed, while she pushed the other woman's head down in there all the way and left it there.

Chapter 11

They stopped. Time to take a breather. Monica needed to rest her tongue and jaw, and the other needed to recover from the intense climaxes.

Some mild kissing of the lips followed, hugging. They sipped their vino, draining the glasses. Then Monica rose, walked to the left side of the spacious room where the tv was, reached inside the entertainment console below for a DVD. Popped it in. Porn. Hardcore porn. Monica had come a long way. What I saw of her, taking a stroll on the wild side years before, had merely been the beginning of her all-out transformation that I had just witnessed a sampling of. Porn was the thing for both these days. I was still contemplating going in there, slapping cuffs on both, taping their mouths shut with duct tape, and dragging them out to the garage where their luxury cars were parked and shoving them in the trunk of one and driving out to the desert to the pre-dug graves.

But I couldn't tear myself away from the scene. I needed to see what else was going down, what else they were about to do to each other. I was making up for lost time: years of going without pussy; years of not only not being able to touch and handle and taste, but not so much as look at the real thing. And now, witnessing it up front, the actual, genuine article, was overwhelming. It was way too incredible to do anything that would cut it short. I only wondered if I'd be able to keep myself from going in there and doing something about the craving and absolute thirst to taste those cunts and butt holes. Could I? Was I able? Did I have the will power?

All those years made it seem nearly impossible to pull off, stay away from. I had to have it; I wanted it. *So goddamn bad it was killing me.* Sweat slid down into my eyes. Part of it was the wool hat; part of it, perhaps the greater part, was the practically uncontrollable need and desire. Even considered, if briefly, drawing the camcorder I'd brought with to shoot footy of the action. But then thought: No. *Absolutely not.* Not what this is about. Two over-the-hill broads engaged in intercourse. It was not easy. Far from it.

Monica took Margie's place on the sofa, and Margie now was the one on her knees, between the other's thighs, spreading them, her tongue darting, looking to service her. Monica's eyes were on the tv screen, watching a couple of large breasted women eating each other out, naked on a wide bed, sixty-nine style.

Margie paused, lifted her head and proceeded to unbutton the other woman's shirt. Helped her out of it, helped her take the bra off, and squeezed and nibbled on her average size breasts, the both of them eyeing what was taking place on the screen from time to time. Although both were turned on by it, you got the idea the porn was there for Margie's benefit primarily, just as her need for it had been blatantly obvious during our trysts back in the day. And before Margie could lower her head back down between Monica's thighs, the phone rang.

Monica reached over to pick it up. Sounded like it was her son. On his way over.

"All right, hon. See you in about an hour." She returned the receiver to the cradle. "It's Modigliani. Stopping by with his girlfriend."

It was decided that they would retreat to one of the bedrooms for act two. There was plenty of time before sonny appeared.

Monica walked to the tv, ejected the DVD, and the two disappeared in the hallway on the right.

Chapter 12

I knew I didn't want to be here when the kid and his girlfriend showed, but neither did I feel like missing out on Monica and Margie's boudoir antics. I wanted to see what else they were up to. There was more to experience for both: them, as well as me: the voyeur/peeper. That's what I was: *effing Peeping Tom.* So be it. Also, I had no plans to harm Monica's son or the girlfriend, either. That was out. I was no serial killer and did not kill at random and/or mindlessly. That was for punks like Manson and the others. Fuck that. Ted Bundy and Dahmer and Jack the Ripper. That was not me. That would never be me. Still had some self-respect. I didn't hurt the innocent. All I was after were the assholes who made me suffer; those who caused me so much grief and discomfort over the years. It was personal. Hurting animals, kids, anyone who did nothing to me, did not hurt me in any way, was out. Did this attitude make me a saint? Was I Mother Teresa suddenly? Was I Christ-like? Hardly. Because I still had venom in me, bile, and had a need to taste vengeance. I had wrath that needed release—and nothing short of release would do. And the peeps responsible: Monica, Margie/the two dykes; as well as a porker named Grozewski, would see to it that I got the release. So be it.

I left my spot at the living room sliding glass door, and walked in back in search of access to the bedroom and hoped the window hadn't been locked by them. I could have gone in through either the front or rear door. That would be later. I wanted to watch from the window. Through a crack in the curtain. There was a screen over the window, but the window itself had been left open just a crack, no doubt, for fresh air. When you had cats around fresh air was a must.

I'd never been a cat guy; dogs were my preferred domestic pet, so the odor hit me right away. Had two felines around. Margie's doing. Monica had been a dog lover like me. Stench caused by cats couldn't be mistaken for anything else. I did my best to ignore it. Had to.

Chapter 13

The DVD was inserted into the player here and the image of the naked peeps appeared on the large tv screen as before. Margie and her accommodating lover had shed their street clothes and were in heels at this point, fishnets and the like: crotchless panties. Margie had handcuffed her willing participant to the brass bed at one end and had her positioned on all fours, with the butt sticking out. She had a cat-o'-nine-tails and gave Monica a good one across the buttocks. Monica winced, shaking that muscular rear end. She was older these days, no doubt, but staying fit had paid off. Even Margie looked pretty damned good; had been taking good care of herself ever since getting off the booze and cheese balls. Sure, nowadays she had high end wine during meals, but for the most part, was booze-free and definitely not like she used to be. And that 'Fred' tat she'd had inscribed on her right cheek that time? Modified into their Triple-Threat logo: red lips with the big tongue hanging down I half-wished my own lips were on.

She raised the hand with the cat-o'-nine-tails and gave it to her lover again, putting some force into it this time. Monica's buttocks were streaked red and she was wincing. Not from pain, but pleasure. Or was it a bit of both?

"Are you *cumming* yet, *bitch?*"

"Yes."

"Tell me, then."

"I am, Madam Margie. Do it. Please."

"Shut up and take it, bitch. Take your punishment. Take it and like it, because you have no choice."

"Yes. Spank me; spank me so good. I need this; I so desperately need to be your sex slave . . ." And she was orgasming repeatedly, her body quivering.

Margie may have had the cat-o'-nine-tails in her right hand, but her left was down there between her upper thighs, pleasuring herself with a vibrator, circling and concentrating on that certain area, getting off.

More. Spank me, baby. Spank me now . . .

"You want more? Did I hear you say you want more of the same?"

Monica was nodding her head, shaking her hips from side to side.

"Then say so. Say it loud enough; say it so that I'll know you mean it."

And Monica repeated her request.

"All right, then, honey pie. My ever-loving, insatiable ho."

She whacked her across the butt cheeks. Monica's ass jerked, further indication and sign that it felt so incredibly good for her. Margie raised that whip hand and did it again. Down it came. Across Monica's voluptuous rear. Again and again and again, Monica climaxing with each stroke of the cat-o'-nine-tails.

Chapter 14

Margie had taken a massive dildo and strapped it on.

I was so turned on by it and the ensuing action that my balls had begun to ache. What was I going to do now? Rush in there and rape the bitches? Could I control the two of them? Where were the guns? Their purses were with them, and these modern dames knew how to use those rods. You bet. Also, what bothered me: I may be a killer—this was something I could live with—but I was no *rapo*. As much as I craved vagina and those tight *culos*, I could not allow myself to go in there and commit rape. This was out. *Out.*

Then what? I stood there and suffered; I stood there, panting and sweating and rubbing myself, but not too much, because if I didn't watch it, I'd be shooting sperm inside my pants. Fuck that. No good.

I took my hand away from my groin. If I refused to go in and get some tang, and if I refused to masturbate . . . what the hell was left for an anti-social psycho like me to do?

Chapter 15

At last, Margie collapsed, as did the other one, as her neck was on the stiff side from all the work and energy she had just expended.

I was breathing hard myself. Thanked all the forces above for this bit of respite. And I didn't dare so much as touch my cock; because if I had, I would have been shooting a ton of jizz right inside my boxers. Shit. Fuck. Piss. Unbearable.

Control. You had to have control. It was the impossible task.

Chapter 16

When I looked back up, Margie had positioned herself up against her partner's rear and was about to slide that massive strap-on inside her backside. I noticed Monica's wrists were no longer cuffed to the brass bed and she had inserted a vibrator inside her cunt.

Could I even take it after what I'd just been subjected to? Was it possible? *I wanted to go in there. So help me; I desperately needed to go in there and get some hairy beaver and tight bunghole.* Son of a bitch. I was even having second thoughts about deep-sixing these spineless, two-faced hoes. I was. Scene was that hot.

Was it a waste to waste them? Would it be? Of *cunt*? Of female *culo*? *BJs*? Why not live here with them for a while, get fucked and blown and then do the payback?

How about that? Rape the skanks for a day or two; maybe longer. . . . Yes, but what about Grozewski and Monica's son, and all those other Hollywood motherfuckers who knew them? How would I deal with all that? Ignore the phone when it rang? Not respond to the intercom when peeps pulled up to the gate and pressed the button and asked what's up?— and when they got no answer, went to *Five-0* and filed a missing persons report, or worse: got someone to break into the place. . . .

No. That was out. Hanging around was out. Too bad, too. Ballbusters had to be dealt with. Sans sex. No fornication; no intercourse. Period. About the only kind of intercourse that takes place will be verbal.

Huh?

Yes.

Verbal.

Fuck verbal. I wanted cunt juice on my lips and tongue; butt hole to smell and taste. I needed it so damned bad. To make up for lost time.

Get a hooker. They're all over the place. Wouldn't be the first time. Get yourself a professional whore. Do it. There cannot be rape here with these two double-crossing wenches.

Chapter 17

While they were orgasming and gasping, I was battling my own situation: impossibly painful case of *blue balls* and *gas build up.* Not only could I not take a step without suffering incredible pain in my loins, but a powerful fart escaped my hind end. I froze still, stiff, fearing they might have heard it.

"Was that you, Marge?"

"Huh?"

"You just fart?"

"No way."

Both were lying on their backs, spent and exhausted.

"Modi and his girlfriend Lucy are on their way over, you know? We probably should shower and get dressed."

Then Margie mentioned Bruno Grozewski and that he and his boyfriend had this actor friend named Bix Dixon they thought would make a good Alf Reed."

"Bix Dixon? He's kind of effeminate, isn't he? Fred may have been many things: creepo, misogynist, liar, thief, anti-social, two-timing a-hole, but no way was he ever gay or show any signs of it, Margie. I can't see spending time reading an actor like Bix who is so blatantly gay."

"What're you got against gay peeps?"

Monica looked at her, then looked away with a smile on her face. Both were staring up at the ceiling.

"I can't do that to him, Marge. Besides, Bix is Jewish."

"Jewish? What's that got to do with anything, Monica? I never knew you to be anti-Semitic."

"I am not anti-Semitic."

"Sounds like it. When you talk like that."

"Oh, stop it."

"Just teasing you, hon."

"I feel guilty as it is. He's been punished enough."

"Punished? Fred? What he got he got because he deserved it. *Fuck him.* If this gay kid can act, let's give him a chance. What would it hurt to just have him come in and read?"

"He does gay porn on the side, Marge. If it got out it would hurt the production."

"Gay porn? Since when are you against gay porn? You can't get enough of it. Something I could never understand: a gay woman getting off on watching *men* fuck each other."

"I wasn't always into girls." Monica was back looking at her lover again. "Didn't even know I had that in me . . . until we met and. . . . I'm glad you're in my life, babe. . . ."

Margie turned on her side, slid her right arm under the other's neck and gave her partner a peck on the cheek.

"Is this the best, or what? Are we lucky? To have each other, to be living in this wonderful house and have the wonderful careers we have: respected by the industry."

Monica said nothing for a while.

"We are. We've come a long way . . . but to cast a known gay porn star to play Fred would not only be so wrong, but probably result in irreparable damage to the film. Not to mention . . ."

"What?"

"He wouldn't stand for it. There is no way Fred would let us get away with it. He's out, and we have no idea where he is even. He could be scheming right now how to get back at us."

"I wouldn't worry about it."

"You don't think he's been scheming the whole time he was in prison

34

how to get back at us? He's the type who loves to harbor a grudge, and he's got a temper. Let's not forget that. It's no joke. I saw it, lived with it. At first, didn't think much of it; didn't let it bother me or worry me. In fact, I found it kind of amusing . . . the way he would get worked up about things: if we were stuck in traffic, or if we were in line to see a bank teller or the grocery line we happened to be in wasn't moving fast enough for him; he just had no patience for these things. And living in L.A, waiting is just a fact of life. He had a tendency to snap. It got to worry me; I'd never been around someone like this. And then he lied to me about his background, childhood. Wouldn't talk about it; would never discuss it with me; refused to."

Margie sat up.

"I still have no idea what you're getting at."

"I'm saying I'd feel better if we got a big dog, couple of them. Maybe hire a guard, at least until Grozewski can figure out where he is. Because right now, we have no idea. None."

Margie reached inside her purse. Withdrew a *Glock*. Checked to make sure it was loaded.

"I got my guard and big dog right here. I hope he comes around and gives me a reason to waste his sorry butt. He's a miscreant; just like Frank Graham. Couple of losers. One is dead, and the other should be. The only mistake we made: not smoking his ass when we had the chance."

Monica looked at her, and didn't seem to like what she was hearing.

"I mean it, Monica. The only reason you have that worried look in your eyes: because the asshole is out there somewhere and he's a threat. And he'll always be a threat, so long as he's not where he belongs: locked up behind bars—or dead."

"You just made my point."

"I need a shower."

"Was he scapegoated?"

"Was *who* scapegoated, Monica?"

"Who are we talking about?"

"*Fred?* He was not. He was determined to take Frank out. I did my best to talk him out of it. He was obsessed. Again, some stupid male ego thing. Had to have me all to himself. You know how they are. Got to own you. It's about ownership with these assholes. There was no way to stop him at the time. I was in love with him and had little choice but to go along. Had Rinelle's life been threatened by Jamal and his druggie vermin due to what she owed them? Of course. I did what I could to get Frank to send money. You know the rest. It's psychologically, as well as emotionally draining to keep going over it. Rinelle played with fire and she got burned. It was love/hate with us. There were things, character traits that I absolutely loathed about her; times I wanted to beat the shit out of her, and did my best—and yet, there's no denying woman did raise me; did what she could with me and my siblings. In her own twisted way, mind you. And we don't want to discuss what went on there. It's too much—and does not make me feel good at all, babe. Just talking about this makes me ache for a long, hot shower. I am not kidding, girlfriend."

Margie had delivered that last line with a smile. Stood up. Dropped the piece back inside her purse, and walked out of the room with it.

"I better take one myself."

And no sooner had Monica said it, did another fart escape my backside. I could have died. Saw her freeze. She was certain she'd heard it this time. Walked over to the window, parted the curtain. Slid the window open wide enough. Had her face up against the screen, looking to her left, then the right. I'd ducked down in time, and held my breath. After a while, she closed and locked the window and drew the curtain shut. Since there was no reason to hold back with the gas anymore, I let go with a whole series of emissions.

Chapter 18

I was at their back door. Inserted the key. Went in. I was ready: had the cuffs, rubber mallet, black hoods, .357 Mag—should I need to shoot my way out.

Cat odor was much stronger now that I was inside and it took a lot more to deal with it. I made it down the corridor, walking on the thick, spotless white carpeting. I looked down, to see if my sneakers left prints, anything *Five-0* might be able to use against me later in court (should I fail in my own demise). Bits of grass, tiny gravel pebbles. Fuck it. Nothing I could do there, not that it was evidence of anything, either.

I looked up at the walls on either side: lined with framed posters and stills, pics of crew, Monica and Margie's friends; Hollywood actors & turds alike. Meant nothing to me.

Door on my left was the bedroom where the divas had been fucking a moment ago. I went in. Mallet at the ready. I would have preferred doing this with a real hammer, but the resulting blood might've worked against me: I did not want to leave this kind of evidence behind. I did not want to create a mess—if I could help it. Do it like before, when I whacked Graham in his hospital bed years before: knock 'em out with the mallet, cuff their wrists behind their back, slip the hoods over their noggins & carry them out, one at a time, to one of their luxury cars; drop them in the trunk, and drive off the property. That would be nice; that would be the ideal for me.

Could I do it? Would it happen? One just never knew how something like this would turn out.

Chapter 19

I went in. Could hear the shower going through the closed bathroom door. Monica was in there. I stood there, and waited. Looked at the messed bed, and walked over. Leaned in, had my nose against the sheet-covered mattress, sniffing, taking hard sniffs; inhaling the aroma. I buried my face in it. Lifted my head; grabbed one of the sheets and held it to my mouth. Inhaled deeply. I could not get enough. And as I did it, I was acutely aware that this did not, in any way, help ease the pain in my nutsack caused by the blue balls.

So why then was I being such a *pervert*? Could not be helped. Too many years gone without pussy; too damned many years. Once again, I found myself entering the john, should the door be unlocked, and there was no reason for it to be locked, smacking her across the face or back of the skull with the mallet, and taking her right there in the shower; having my fill, then dragging her out to the bed, and leaving her there long enough to go take care of the other whore.

Would I? Did I dare? Was I a *rapo* at heart? No. Couldn't lower myself to the level of the rapos I'd met in the joint. Fucks were hated; rapos and pedophiles. They got their asses kicked up and down the fucking yard. More than a few ended up getting shivved in the kidneys or guts. Left to bleed to death.

Fuck this kind of thinking. I was on a mission. Get to it. I did notice their panties on the carpeting. Picked those up, took my whiffs, and jammed them in my back pocket for later masturbatory fantasies. Why not? Jerking it was not a favorite thing, not after having done it for years in the joint, but it still beat sexual assault.

I was at the door to the john. Turned the knob, and went in. Shower was still going strong. I could see her body through the quasi clear shower curtain. The thing had flower patterns on it and it was the reason she hadn't picked up that I was there; that and the fact she was shampooing her hair and face.

I found the piece in her purse. Jammed it in my hip pocket. I reached out with my left hand toward the shower curtain, about to grab it and yank back, while the other that I held the mallet in rose and rose, above my head. This was going to be a beauty: a hard smack down swing that would knock her out and drop her to the bottom of the tub. Except the damned phone rang. And rang. Shit. It startled me. Threw me. I had to get out of there.

Chapter 20

I stood in the bedroom, just outside the john door, listening—as she talked on the phone. It was then I noticed I had failed, better yet, had not been able to close the john door after I'd stepped out. There hadn't been time. I heard her stop talking. It was then I thought I had better duck behind the bed. I hurried over to the far side, and dropped to my belly, just as she stuck her head out through the open bathroom door to take a look around. She must have realized it was odd. She must have thought she'd closed the door earlier, only to discover that it had been left ajar.

I heard her close the john door, and step back inside and continue her conversation on the phone. I had no idea how long she'd be on that damned phone, and got out of there. Walked down the corridor, to a door on my right, another bedroom, and went in. If I couldn't get Monica right now, I'd take care of that bitch Margie first, then return to fix her pal.

"Margie," I heard Monica call her co-conspirator through the closed bedroom door I'd just left. There was a door directly across the way, to a walk-in closet, and I ducked in there in time, leaving the door ajar from fear the noise it would make if I'd attempted to close it. Monica called her 'wife's' name again, as she walked down the hallway to the room Margie was in. I listened intently.

"Phone call for you, Margie hon."

Monica stuck her head into the bedroom, then she returned to the bedroom she had come from. Closed the door.

I eased out of the closet. Entered Margie's room. Neat, clean. Framed pics. All sorts. Friends and family members. Some of her stepfather Mario. Even one or two of Rinelle.

I walked up to the closed bathroom door. Could hear Margie talking on the phone through the noise caused by the shower. She hung up the phone eventually, then stepped in the shower. I had my hand on the door knob, and turned it, attempting to get in there. Only the door was locked. *Locked.* Fuck.

I had a choice, force it in—and risk getting shot—or show some patience? I'd waited this long, what was a while longer? What difference would it make? I'd get them; I knew this for a fact. I'd get both bitches and make them pay. Only I wanted to get in there so bad I could taste it.

I'd had lousy luck in getting to Monica, now I was experiencing the same kind of bullshit with her cunt roommate.

At least I had one of their guns; I had Monica's weapon. All I had to do was get Margie's. That would be it. Unless they had a few more lying around. Just never knew with these modern day violent femmes who loved guns. It was like fucking Annie Oakley or something. Broads never used to go for guns, unless they were old and wrinkled; now those bitches usually packed, on account they had no choice, but these younger babes never did. This was a new one; modern day obstacles for homeys like me to have to deal with. I didn't like it; didn't care for it—but there it was.

Chapter 21

Made me wonder who they'd been talking to? Who else was on the way besides Monica's son Modigliani and Lucy? Grozewski and his boyfriend and their protege Bix? I didn't know; hadn't been able to make out the phone chats through the closed doors.

What now? Take the one out? Monica, and risk undue trouble when Margie starts looking for her? I wanted both—with as little risk as possible. Not only did I want both, but I had to have Grozewski as well. I needed the trio. All three—or nothing. I didn't expect to get Grozewski while here, but at the least, I needed to get the two bitches.

This was a situation now. Also, it occurred to me, Monica would eventually realize that her gun was missing.

I decided to get the fuck out of the bedroom, especially when I heard Monica's bedroom door open again, and Monica calling Margie's name.

I was in the kitchen part, standing there, waiting, listening.

"You take my gun?" They were in Margie's bedroom now. I could hear them both plain enough.

"Your gun? Why would I do that? Why would I even go in your purse? You know we don't do that sort of thing around here."

"Oh, God. This is not good."

"What are you saying?"

"I am saying I am not in the habit of misplacing my guns."

"Could it be possible that this time —"

"No, Margie."

"Okay. What about your keys? You don't recall what happened there, am I right?"

Both were quiet during the next moment, silent. Then I heard a noise like a safe being opened, a gun being cocked. Shit. All I needed; two suspicious ballbusters with loaded guns.

I could have easily shot it out with them, traded bullets and vamoosed. But I didn't want it that way. It would have alerted Bruno, and *Valley Five-0*, and the hunt for an ex-con named Alfred Lester Reed would have been on, pronto. All points bulletin. Get the lowlife scumbag.

I had no choice, but to get out. Scram. Now. The only way I saw it. No way was I giving up. Merely postponing my plans for payback.

As I made it through the kitchen and reached for the side door, I thought: hold on. Just a second here. Kitchen was spotless, counters clean, not a single dirty dish in the sink. To cause them both a bit of confusion, I decided to leave Monica's piece right there on the counter next to the toaster and the knife rack, right after I hit the clip release and pocketed that, including the round in the chamber.

Sure. Let them mull that one over. Then I reached for the door handle to the large fridge, opened it. Jerked it and shot sperm into the 2% carton of milk. Shook it. Returned it. Then I pissed into the OJ. Shook the bottle some. The encore remained. I dug inside my jacket pocket for the narrow jar of *antifreeze*. Uncapped it, poured enough antifreeze into the wine that was the same shade of rosy red. They had a few bottles in there, all types: white, whatnot. Wine drinkers. Monica always was. Now we were all *triple-threats*, were we not?

I zipped up. Helped myself to a can of *V-8* juice, stepped through a doorway on my left that took me into the laundry room, then made an immediate right. Opened the door there, and stepped outside.

Chapter 22

I made it down the stoop. Pressed my body against the side of the house and drank from the *V-8* can. I waited and listened. Margie was in the kitchen. I knew it was her because I could hear her call Monica's name.

"I want you to see something, honey. *Monica?*"

After a while I heard the other ho.

"No way."

"You never misplace your guns?"

"There is no way I left it there, Margie. It was in my purse, I tell you. *In my purse.* My gun never leaves my purse, unless I intend to use it; as well as when we're at the shooting range. *You know this.*"

"It's possible it was right there all along, honey."

"Something weird is going on. The hallway carpet has some grass and gravel on it that wasn't there before, Marge. Something strange is happening."

"Or else it could be a simple case of mild paranoia."

"This is not funny. Not to me. Not funny at all. My *Glock* did not leave my purse on its own to end up on the kitchen counter. Something is seriously the matter here."

"When you figure out what it is, can you please clue me in?"

"I want to check the grounds."

"Before you do that, better check your Glock to make sure it's loaded."

"You know it's loaded. No point in keeping a gun in my purse unless it's loaded."

"Just check."

Sounded like Monica did.

"Shit. What the fuck is going on? *The clip is gone.* First my keys disappear, now this."

That was the last bit I heard, because I got out of there. Made my way toward the back, all the while thinking: Yes. Let them mull it over.

Garage looked pretty large to me. Big enough for four vehicles. That's what was in there: two M. Benzes, a Vette; one big ass SUV. I needed to find a place to hide out for a while. Maybe for the rest of the night.

Chapter 23

Monica cased the grounds: gun in one hand, flashlight in the other. I could have easily wasted her, then gone inside and taken care of the other twat.

What stopped me? What kept me from doing it? Her son. I didn't want him to see his mother in the kind of condition I was determined to leave her in. Nothing more to it than that. I wasn't about to spread misery beyond my payback plan. So you see, the FBI pros, and other profilers, have it all wrong. Not all anti-social types are alike; not all of us kill in the same manner or for the same reason.

Was it blood lust? To a certain degree. In this case. Some of that in there. And because of my attitude, I couldn't do anything to her . . . unless she left me no choice. Unless it came down to: *her or me.* And if I got cornered, was left without a way out, I'd have to put her butt in the effing ground. Then take care of Margie. And that still would have left fat ass Bruno to deal with.

The other thing that made it worse: I didn't want to have to go back to the dishwashing job; I didn't want to have to listen to any more talk of movies and casting and budgets and locations; I didn't want to have to listen to them talk about how they needed to *'tailor the story'* in order for the movie to work. My own demise would've been easier to take than having to return to *Pinocchio's Pasta.* And I was determined not to. I had no idea how I was going to stick with this resolve, all I knew I was determined.

I kept peeking from behind the SUV. Monica walked cautiously, aiming that flashlight from side to side of the vast yard: the pool area, lounge chairs, barbecue. Then the door opened, and the other lesbian was out, Margie. Had her gun with her, a flashlight. So now I had both to contend with. What chance did I have of getting out without having to put them in the ground right here in their own backyard? And when would Monica's son and his girlfriend show? Wasn't it about time? And who else was on the way? Grozewski and his boyfriend? And that actor they called Bix Dixon?

I had no idea; all I knew was these backstabbing bitches that I hated and loathed and despised were bound to locate my hiding place. As if I didn't have enough to cope with, more gas was struggling to escape my rectum. I needed to fart. Holding one or two farts back, without major consequences was possible, but when you had a series struggling to leave your asshole, it became a pain.

What the fuck was I going to do? Not only about the gas, but the armed bitches who were ready to shoot on sight? They knew how to use those effing rods; I saw the paper targets from the indoor range. They hit the Bull's eye more often than not. Far better shots than me. It was not easy to admit, but hell, it was true. And a guy with a black ski mask on, and the rest of him in black attire, was not about to be mistaken for Saint Nick, especially not this time of year.

I couldn't help it, and released another fart. And a beam of light, probably Monica's, drifted over to my part of the garage. Was I fucked? Would I have to open up? Kill them both, and the hell with the rest of it?

My biggest screwup, miscalculation, so far, since setting foot on the property, was not killing them while inside. This was going to be much tougher. A gun fight was sure to alert the neighbors, and *Five-0* would be on their way. And I'd have a much tougher time getting to Grozewski.

The beam of light shifted away from my area, and was on other parts of the garage.

"You heard that? Margie?"

"What was it?"

Monica said nothing.

"You just make sure you don't shoot me by mistake, Monica. Or the cats."

"*Cats?* Didn't know they were out."

"They got out. Or one did."

"Great."

"Just be careful."

Chapter 24

Either Margie's or her wife's cell went off. Sounded like Margie talking into hers. The cat they mentioned earlier walked past me, startling the holy shit out of me. Not having been able to determine what it was initially, I'd been ready to fill it full of holes. Could have been a raccoon, a dog, possum, anything. I'd had no idea. It was a good thing I'd have been able to keep calm.

Margie was talking. They were both a good distance away, but I could make out some of it. The damned cat walked back this way, and I was able to hiss at it. And it scampered off with a yowl. Then ran out of the garage, toward Monica. I could hear Monica give up a sigh of relief. She scooped the cat up in her arms and walked back toward the house.

"Bruno. Wants to know if it would be all right to stop by with Bix."

I could see Monica shake her head.

"Well?"

"I don't mind doing favors for people, Margie; helping out. . . . I just don't like having my arm twisted to cast someone in a role they're not qualified for."

"How do we know that he's not qualified?" Marge had the phone covered with her free palm, to keep the party at the other end from hearing what was being discussed.

"We've gone over this, Marge. I'm tired of it. It's getting late. My son is coming over. Why can't Bruno's friend stop by the production office instead? Say sometime tomorrow? Why does he need to bring him by here tonight?"

"Feels he would get lost in the shuffle. Hates cattle calls."

"It wouldn't be a *'cattle call.'* We don't treat people like cattle and never have. He can come in by himself and we can read him then."

"Can he at least stop by to pick up the sides?"

"He wants pages? Tonight?"

"So he can prepare, before we have him come in. Bruno is convinced this kid has real talent."

"Where have we heard that one before? Town's full of geniuses."

"Yes or no, Monica? I will go along with whatever you say on this. I can't keep him waiting all night."

I heard Monica curse under her breath.

"Okay. Have them stop by."

Margie spoke into her cell, then ended the conversation.

"Know what this is, don't you? Bruno hung up on another one. By giving him a break, he figures the kid owes him, and he's in his pants. And I get tired of it, Margie."

"Come on."

"How many times has he pulled this? He doesn't seem to give a damn that if an actor is wrong it can kill the movie. Shitty movies get made all the time, and this is just another reason why: *actors who can't fucking act.* I'm sick of it. And besides, looks like we're going to have to go back to producing porn for a while to replenish the coffers."

"I was afraid of that."

"See now why I get upset when Bruno pulls this shit?"

"You're also being unfair about him. He's brought us some pretty darn good people, too, over the years. Male and female talent."

"Know what? I'm tired of discussing it."

It was at this point that a tan van drove up to the wrought iron gate. Margie chin-gestured in its direction.

"Looks like Modi's here."

Chapter 25

The sliding gate alone looked like it must've cost a few grand by itself.
Way more than the crappy van I owned, that was for sure. They were doing all right. I should've been impressed. Truth was very little impressed me at this point. That gate was on a rail and you could hear it crawling along, sliding open. There was Modi in the fancy van with the big ass mag wheels waiting for the gap to widen enough to drive through. It took a while, but the opening was finally adequate and the son drove on through and took the road in and pulled up to where Monica and Margie were waiting.

The driver climbed down. Modigliani was in his late 20s these days, a healthy looking, handsome dude. Chick magnet. Like I used to be. Way back when. A blond stepped down from the passenger side. She was in heels, long legs. Had some type of sexy dress on with a slit. Woman was stacked, from what I could tell.

I could hear Monica's son introduce the woman with him to his mother, then to Margie, and the four of them went in the house.

There was a door on my right with a sign on it that said: **Studio**. I hadn't noticed that before. I'd taken this part of the structure to be the guest house or maid's quarters, and maybe at one time it could have been—but the sign said it was a studio. It made sense, in that Monica and her partner were filmmakers. Well, let's say they were involved in it. To call them 'filmmakers' might be giving them more credit than they deserved. My take on it. The way I saw it.

I turned the knob, and went in. Turned my penlight on, and waved it around. Carefully, cautiously. There were video cameras on tripods, a Nagra audio recorder on a table and some other video-related equipment: slate boards, rolls of duct tape, markers. One section of the set-up was made up to look like a bedroom, in that there was a brass bed and three false walls. Wall on the left side, and one on the right. Plus the one directly behind the headboard. Front of the bedroom was wide open for camera access. There were some fake plants, framed crappy paintings, end tables, lamps. There was a unisex john to my right. I noticed a Coke machine. Your average kitchen type refrigerator. Had me wondering if there was anything edible in there. Also had me wondering if I might be able to hide out here for a while? Long enough to take care of business: hammer the trio in the skull, dump them in one of the vehicles and drive them out to the desert. This way I wouldn't have to return to the furnished room, wouldn't have to put in another day at the Pinocchio diner. Just stay here and take it easy. And if there wasn't enough food in this fridge, all I'd have to do is wait for the bitches to leave the house, and make myself at home. Eat their food, shit, shower and take it easy—all the while working out how to carry out what I needed. Work on perfecting the plan. Execute it when I was ready.

I walked over to the fridge. Had my hand on the door handle. And just as I was about to open the door, I heard voices approaching. The lot of them were walking up to the studio, not through the garage, but the other door that was in the front.

Shit. I had to scramble and hide. Where? I hadn't really had enough time to scope out this part of the joint. There were plenty of places to duck and hide, only I hadn't been able to consider; and now I did not have the needed time. So I dove under the bed. Crawled under and away, toward the back wall.

I'd remain balled up in my all black attire and wait to see what happened. If I got found out I got found out. I'd crawl out and let the fireworks commence. Fuck it.

The front door opened.

Chapter 26

Monica and Margie walked in. One of them flicked the light switch on the wall. The place lit up, everywhere but under the bed. I hoped so, anyway. I could see them, all of them; from their feet up to their heads. For the time being. Once they started to walk toward the center the heads went, got cropped, then shoulders, and so on, until all I could see of them was from the feet up to as far as their knees, then even lower than that.

That blond with Modigliani was built like a brick shit house. She was a coed interested in doing adult flicks to pay her way through college, from what I gathered. Could be it was bull crap, but this was the line she stuck to. So Monica's kid was a procurer now, unless Lucy, the coed's name, was not a true girlfriend, instead merely Lay of the Week. Didn't matter. Because they were discussing her maybe doing a masturbation video at first, to see how she liked it. If she felt comfortable, then take it from there.

Monica was doing the talking. In charge. At least here. Playing the in-control director. Back in the bedroom with all those carnal antics, she was the slave, taking orders from Marge. Not here, not now.

"What do you think?"

Seemed she was asking the woman her son had introduced as Lucy earlier.

"I would like that."

"So long as it's understood: You will never be asked to do anything you're not comfortable with. I know certain unscrupulous types out there behave that way. We don't. Marge and I don't care for any of that underhanded bullshit that certain video companies like to pull on those new to the industry."

"That's what Modi was telling me. And that's exactly why I'm here. I feel good about the whole thing."

"Have you considered a stage name, honey?"

"Not really."

She asked where the woman was born.

"Anchorage."

"How does Lucy Ice sound to you?"

"Why not?"

"You will not be asked to fuck anyone you don't feel like fucking, Lucy Ice. You will not be asked to eat out anyone, blow anyone, you don't absolutely feel comfortable with. You need anything: like lube, to drink; whatever, you don't hesitate to let us know. People who work for us, rather in our productions, are treated fairly and with respect every step of the way."

I got it. This foxy, hot cunt was going to take her clothes off and masturbate on the bed, and I wouldn't be able to see it. It bothered me; I think it bothered me even more than having to hide out in this chicken shit manner from the hoes I'd come to abduct and haul off to the pre-dug holes in the ground I had waiting out there for them.

Chapter 27

Okay. There were mirrors throughout the place, all types: on casters, framed, you name it, as well as other props. Mirrors made trick shots possible, as well as certain porn performers liked to watch themselves while fucking and/or chugging sperm. I understood; and just wished they'd taken the time to adjust one of those mirrors so that I might be able to watch this babe play with her tits and pussy.

But they were at it, and didn't give a shit about my needs one damned bit. Guess I was still human, after all; vengeful, blood lust on the brain, slaughter-bound—and yet I still wanted to see what was about to go down with this hottie and her steaming cunt.

They got some kind of easy beat going; the usual synthesizer porn mood music. Coed Lucy stood on the floor, doing a slow dance number. It was pretty much easy to surmise: swaying those hips from side to side, bending over, cupping those large hooters, and then squeezing them together. Only all I could see was the lower part of those tanned calves and the feet in those black stiletto heels. Her toenails had been painted with cherry red nail polish. Monica was giving gentle instructions: Turn this way, honey; now that way.

"Stick your tongue out, sweetie. Now lick your lips. Upper, then lower; slowly . . . take your time. That's it; take your sweet time. You're making love to the camera. Actually you're getting the middle-aged jerk with the beer belly watching this horny as hell." Then she corrected herself. "I shouldn't be saying that." She laughed. "You're enticing a really hot, studly guy with a major boner right now. . . . Your hands are inside your upper thighs; gently, gradually, rubbing . . . not quite on your cookie, but near it, around it: above, along the sides, and below, but not on it . . . not yet. . . ."

They were destroying me. I couldn't see it, but it was easy to imagine what was going on. Then the thing I dreaded might happen was taking place: Monica was asking her to bend forward, all the way, and touch her ankles. . . . While the blond did this, I could see her face. . . . Had she been paying any attention at all, she would have spotted me, discovered me, and I would have been in deep *crapolla*.

Monica asked her to turn around, so that her ass was to the camera; run her hands up, up up along the sides of her legs, lift the dress up and over her buttocks, to reveal the thong panties. I couldn't see that; all I could make out was the back of the woman's head and all that blond hair hanging there.

"Slow, always, slowly run the palms of your hands over your buns . . . have them linger there. Gently, caressing your butt crack with the tips of your fingers. . . . Please take your time. Keep the tips of your fingers there, up and down, slowly, slowly. . . . Now, take that hand and rest it on your right hip. Take your other hand, and slide it from in front of your pelvis and gently rub the mound. . . . Rub the cloth over the pussy. . . . Rub it . . . rub it. . . ."

My cock was hard. There was no way to keep it from happening.

Chapter 28

She was done stripping and needed to take a pee break. That's what was heard. And me? I had a far worse problem: my bowels needed evacuating, on top of the gas situation. Yes, I needed to take a shit, bad. And there was no fucking way.

Some goddamn vengeful, tough-ass mofo. That was me. Stuck under a bed in a makeshift porn studio in somebody's backyard needing to take a dump—and not able to budge. Huh? While everyone else took their break, drinking *Perrier* or *Pepsi* or root beer. What?

They were discussing the second phase. What to do next. She was going to be inserting an impressive dildo in her cunt, and maybe something up her butt, too. Some type of butt plug, something. And then, for phase three, they wanted her to shave her *vagina*. That was their word, not mine. I rarely use 'vagina' when talking about pussy. I prefer cunt, twat, beaver, snatch or snapper. Anything but vagina.

But yes, they were going to have her shave, especially if that effeminate actor friend of Bruno's was coming over. Maybe they could have him do a scene with this Lucy hottie. Maybe. Yes, the guy appeared in gay male films, but you never knew: it was possible he'd be able to get it up for Lucy. There were types who swung both ways: did men and babes. They'd have to see.

Lucy Ice was back. I could hear those high heels hitting parts of the cement floor. Some of the cement was covered with rugs, not all, but some of it, especially in and around the bed.

Monica's cell went off. She spoke into it. Bruno was at the gate. Somebody needed to go out there with a remote and let the man in. Modigliani volunteered. His mother handed him the remote and he left.

The music was back on. Lucy was on the bed. I could hear her writhing and moving about up there above me. Monica wanted sighs and moans, but nothing fake.

"Keep in mind, hon, less is more. Always, darling. *Less is more.* Tone it down. It can be intense, so long as you're feeling it and are able to convey this to us."

The whore's moans decreased, but the movement went on, the vibrator was humming.

"In and around the clit, sweetie; slowly, gently, mouth open; you're looking at the camera. . . . Look into the camera, not me, the camera. That's it, sweetie. Mouth stays open, head back some. . . . It's on the clit. It stays there. . . . Now, gradually, gradually . . . down, down, lower and lower, slide it inside. . . . Slowly, in . . . and slowly, out. . . . That's it. . . ."

The door opened, and in walked Bruno and his protege, the gay porn actor. Yes. Quite the stud: tall, dark and handsome. Only it's going to be interesting to see if he can get it up for this Lucy hottie. I wished I was in his shoes so I could fuck the shit out of her right now; jump her effing bones and drill her asshole, then her snatch, up into her mouth, and back down again . . . way inside that rectum. My dick was hard, and the gas wanted out; as did something else.

Now the talent was being told to reach for the butt vibrator and insert that up her shitter. Damn, I wanted to see this. It was a real bitch not being able to move, not being able to do something about it.

I could see Bruno and his boy Bix standing out there, expressionless. It didn't work for them. Big tits; sweet, tight twat meant nothing. Zippo. Zero. They were into something else. Effing Bruno's mind was on what this guy Bix was packing down there.

What a topsy-turvy world we lived in. A hot ho like Lucy up there probing her tight asshole with a vibrator, another in her moist cunt, and these guys were *nonplussed*. I didn't get it. I mean I did—but I really didn't.

How could they not be interested, at least to some degree? How was that possible? Bruno had even been married, with kids! Forget it, amigo. You ain't about to solve a damned thing.

Chapter 29

Lucy Ice was instructed to take the vibrator out of her cunt and slide it up across her belly, between her tits and up into her mouth. Run the tip of her tongue around the crown, always taking her time, then slide the thing into her mouth and suck on it.

"That's it, dear. Suck it. . . ."

After a while, it was back down at her pussy. She was instructed to turn over, on her knees, ass in the air, and continue . . . and take it home. Monica requested a prolonged and protracted orgasm, a series of them. She wanted Lucy's body to quake and quiver; she needed her to wince.

Lucy was wincing and something additional: gasping and groaning, moaning. I got the idea Monica was having her replay her very own orgasms back in the bedroom with her partner Margie—by proxy.

And then it was over. This part of it, anyway.

Monica thanked the girl, and suggested she was free to shower. Lucy walked off toward the john, and Monica and Margie turned to Bruno and his young pal Bix. Intros were made all around.

He was handed his sides from their upcoming crime drama 'loosely' based on my life, and given time to go over them, before doing a reading with either Margie or Monica, maybe even Modi.

Chapter 30

Lucy was back, still in those stiletto heels, and she had a white terrycloth, knee length robe on. Hair combed, lipstick red mouth, and smelling like tulips. She sat in one of the chairs at the far end, legs crossed, smoking a cigarette.

Bix seemed to be ready. He sat in a canvas chair across from Margie. Margie would be the one doing the scene with him. Monica was directing, as usual. Her son was running the camera. They were videotaping the reading.

Well, Bix delivered his lines and he was so effing bad that I nearly cursed out loud and jumped out from under the bed. Fuck this gay porn actor. *Fuck him.* He sucks. And I don't mean dick, either. Not this time. Can't act. And I didn't want him playing me. Period. He was awful. Just plain awful. Yes, it was merely a cold reading; I knew a bit about these things from having been around Monica and Margie listening to all the chatter at the diner; still, even I knew enough to know that the punk was a dud.

Yes; okay; he was probably hung like a rhino, but he couldn't act worth a shit. Get rid of him, I nearly blurted out. Tell him to take a hike. Now. Please. Please don't let him play me. Anyone but him. *Anyone.*

Chapter 31

The scene was over, thank god. Over. Even Monica, bless her, could see that the guy was no good. As an actor, anyway. So did Margie; so did everyone in the room except Bruno.

"What do you think, Monica?"

People were quiet. This was the way it went when someone was lousy; didn't have it. Bruno needed his answer. Reminded Monica she ought to give him one.

"Well?"

"Bruno, you're a friend, a great friend. We've known each other for years . . . ."

"But what?"

"The best we can do is offer him video work."

"Porn? He's trying to get away from it. He wants to be a legitimate actor. That's why I brought him over. I thought you'd understand."

"I do. We do."

"Who's 'we'?"

"Margie and I."

"I don't hear Margie saying anything."

"I back her, Bruno."

"Just like that. It's *cold reading*, for Christ's sake. He didn't even have a chance to prepare, Monica."

"You wanted it this way, Bruno."

"He's under pressure. This is real pressure here. Bix is good. I've seen him work. And I don't mean what he does in those smut videos. He's great in them; but I mean the kid, Bix, can act. I think he's a real thespian. Maybe not in Olivier's league, or Brando's, but in there somewhere, for sure."

"You see, exactly why I was against this. I did not want this, my friend. Bruno, this is no good; this is not right. Sorry, Bix."

The fat man sighed. Yes, Bix didn't look happy, but whose fault was that? He had talent in a different area. Let it go at that. Should have been pleased. I mean, the motherfucker had a big dick, from all accounts. Be happy. I wasn't small myself; wasn't huge, but this guy certainly had to have more than me. So why not take it and cheer up? Make your money, if you're doing smut, or else get the fuck out and go deliver pizza or wash dishes. I did it; many of the dead-end, low-wage shit jobs. In and out of prison. Was he too good? Evidently.

Margie had an idea: why didn't they take a break? Go in the house and have a sandwich, a cocktail, and talk it over like adults?

Yes, I said. To myself.

Chapter 32

As soon as they left, turned out the light, I was out from under that bed and rushing into the john. Dropped my pants and shat like a champ. Goddamn. What a relief.

I mean, yes, sex was great, and love was great (the rare times it worked) and other things were great and mattered, but if you couldn't take a shit when you really needed to, you were effing dead. Same thing if you couldn't whiz. I remembered what Graham went through at the VA that time. Stuck in a nightmare of escalating agony. So, this was the best break I'd had in a while: being able to empty my bowels and ponder my next move.

There was a shelf, 20 feet wide or something and looked about 6 ft. deep, right above the bed, where a bunch of props were kept. A wooden ladder ran up from the floor along the right side wall. What if I explored that part of the studio to see if I could find a place to hide out for the time being?

I wiped, showered, got into my skins. There were toothbrushes there, but I didn't dare use any of them. Hey, they had effing porn stars in this place, peeps who licked each other's cornholes—and I sure as hell was not about to use a toothbrush used by these mooks.

I pulled the ski mask over my face and stepped out of the john. My belly reminded me I was both: hungry and thirsty. I was back at the fridge. I didn't care for Perrier, but that was what was in there, so I grabbed a bottle, uncapped it, and took a long pull. There was a brick of Swiss cheese wrapped in plastic that looked inviting. I grabbed it, tore the plastic cover off and took a bite. A couple of slices of bread would've been perfect, but you can't have everything. Cheese hit the spot. I chased it with another pull of Perrier.

I walked over to the ladder. Paused there. Looking up at the shelf. Could it hold me? Could the shelf support my weight? On top of all else that was up there? And what if one of them should appear looking for something, dildos and whatnot, and discovered my ass hiding in there? Simple: they'd get their ass shot off. Bang bang. No worry.

I could hear them out there, walking up to the door. What choice did I have? Back under the bed, or upstairs? I'd had enough of being under the damned bed like a rodent, and climbed up that ladder as fast as I was able.

The door opened and the bunch entered. I ducked down, crawled along the creaking, dust and cobweb covered boards to a spot behind a cardboard box full of all sorts of porn paraphernalia and froze and hoped the racket I'd made hadn't been heard by them.

Chapter 33

If I'd thought I was in a precarious situation, and no doubt, I was: concerned that the boards might not be able to support my weight, or that if I moved so much as an inch, the creaking would alert the Hollywood geniuses below—someone else was experiencing a far greater dilemma. The big, bad stud horse couldn't perform. He got out of that robe he had on, stood there: 6ft 3, 18-inch arms, narrow waist, washboard abs; all that, plus the thick hunk of meat, and he couldn't get it up. Had to hand it to Bruno, though, in that he never wavered in his support.

"Give him a chance."

So they did. Let him climb on the bed and try to make it with the voluptuous Lucy. Margie and Modi videotaped what was taking place. Only not much was going on, in that the 'Great Adonis' Bix Dixon stayed limp.

Monica was cursing under her breath. Bruno was about to open his mouth again, and she raised her hand to tell him to zip it. But they continued taping. This bastard couldn't even fake liking to lick pussy. *WTF?* I could see the expression of disgust on his face. What kind of porn actor can't even fake liking beaver and tits? Lucy was frustrated. Took offense. Who could blame her? Not I.

Finally Bix Nix (what his name should have been) sat up, apologizing.

"I'm sorry. I truly am sorry, Ms. Gooch. I wanted so much to do my best for you, for my friend Bruno. I . . ." He shook his head, and began to cry. His face in his hands and he wept.

Fuck. I felt sorry for the gay Terminator. I did. What could you do? Pussy was not his thing. Some men, like this stud, were into dick. Dudes. Cock and balls.

Someone handed him a tissue. I think it was Monica, who walked over and put her arm around his shoulders.

"Now, now. . . . None of that."

She walked him away from the bed, and for something to do, they resumed shooting more footy of Lucy jerking herself. Yes, get as much as we can of this young ingenue, and the goddamned boards beneath me, even though I hadn't moved a fraction of an inch, cracked by degrees and gave, and down I dropped, right beside the blond bimbo; and the legs on the bed broke, and the bed hit the floor. Miraculously enough, I'd managed to hold on to the Perrier and Swiss cheese. Proved how empty my belly was. And for lack of a better idea, as I was stunned myself, just as Lucy and everyone else was, I rolled over and dug my face between Lucy's thighs and began lapping cunt as if my life depended on it. Because it did. I was scared shitless—but there was nothing else I could think of.

Lucy had screamed and screamed some more. Monica, had the situation under control, and demanded that her son and Margie continue filming. She was acting as though the whole thing had been planned.

"Remember, hon: *less is more*. You're doing just great, Lucy. Keep doing what you're doing."

Lucy settled down, and her moans by this point were genuine, because I'd pulled the ski mask back, off of my face, and was eating the hell out of her. I was desperate, and what kept me desperate was knowing that both Margie and Monica were packin'. And I had no idea how I was going to talk my way out of this.

Chapter 34

The young ingenue was orgasming, one after another. Enough of that, I thought. I needed to get mine, and I maneuvered myself up toward her mouth, slid it in there. Fuck it. If I was busted, I might as well bust a nut.

She went to it. Dumb blond college bimbo, was sucking with enthusiasm. And they were getting it on tape. That was all that mattered; and I knew I'd have to have some kind of explanation when it was all over. What was I going to say? I had no idea, either.

I made sure Ms. Ice didn't overlook a bit of the region. I had a bite of that Swiss cheese, pulled on the bottle. She worked the helmet. Ran her tongue over and circled. Now, I thought. Here it is: I'm blasting. A Fred Reed *tsunami*. I unloaded. And kept going. The ingenue was desperate for this job and future work, and never wavered on the enthusiasm. Good. Great.

I screamed. It was amazing. Nearly choking on the chunk of cheese in my throat. Managed to recover. When I looked up, I could see that Bruno was too pissed to appreciate what had just taken place. He and his young stud muffin walked to the door and were gone. The scene was over. Lucy asked the director for permission to shower.

"Of course, darling."

Monica waited for the girl to go in the john, then turned to me. I made a half-hearted attempt to pull the mask back down, but it didn't work. She had her gun in her fist, so did Margie.

"Now, who the fuck are you, buster? And what the fuck are you doing hiding out in our studio?"

I was ordered to ditch the ski mask. Did that. Then pulled down my collar, to reveal the prison neck scar. Silently requested pen and paper in order to write. Was given it, and I jotted down that I had been desperate to break into porn and thought this would be the only way that I could show that I was capable; I was also homeless, and finally asked for their forgiveness.

Due to the heavy beard, and deep sunburn, they hadn't been able to figure out who I was, or could they? I figured it wouldn't be long before they finally got it. Of course, if they didn't, there was always Monica's son, who might. True enough, I'd met him years ago and the kid had been in his early teens back then and we had spent next to zero time in each other's company the times he came by to visit his mother, still. . . .

"You're good, did a nice job there, but who are you? We still need to know who you are, what your background is, before we can even consider signing you. You can't just walk in off the street and expect to be hired."

Margie was shaking her head. "Fuck all that." She demanded to see some ID.

I was screwed.

Lucy emerged from the restroom, and I pleaded for them to let me use the john, that I desperately needed to take a leak. They couldn't refuse me. I had some more of that Perrier, another bite of cheese, and placed both gingerly on the night stand. Gesturing with my hands, I promised I'd answer all of their questions right after I took care of business in the john.

Chapter 35

I hurried in there, opened the small window, and crawled through. It was a task, because these things are usually narrow. But I managed somehow. The only thought on my mind was to get to the wall, scale it, and jump to the other side and scram.

I got to the top, when I heard them yelling for me to stop. All were out. Margie and Monica aiming those Glocks. Would they fire? *They wouldn't; they couldn't.* Neighbors would hear the shots and call the bulls. This would not make them popular. Add the fact you're making porn in a residential neighborhood. Not against the law necessarily. It was private property after all, but just a bit uncouth—even in uber liberal Porn Valley. About the only thing that kept my ass from taking a bullet. These wenches were good shots. I made it over.

"We don't want to wake the neighbors." It was Margie. Reminding her wife.

"It was him."

"You sure?"

"It's fucking Fred! It was him!"

"But the beard. I couldn't tell. I mean there was something about him but I . . . I don't know. . . ."

"Call Valley PD. The asshole is back. He's the dishwasher at *Pinocchio's.*"

"Redd Dogg?"

"Yes."

"Exactly! That's why that face looked familiar."

"He was there all those times, ever since his release, snooping around, scheming how to get in here, cause us trouble."

"He said he had no place to go."

"He also claimed he couldn't speak. When you and I both know he can. Sounded hoarse, caused by whatever happened to him in prison, but we both heard him talk in the diner, Margie. *You know we did!*"

"Why did he have to come by here? Why couldn't he stay away and leave us be? We want nothing to do with him and he knows this. And yet, he had enough balls to come by and harass us. Unreal. The way he fell through the boards like that. *Fucking too much.*"

"We better stock up on ammo. With that asshole around. He's trouble; always has been. He'll do his best to turn our lives upside down. I know him. What did I tell you about his vindictive nature? He holds a grudge. He's blaming us for his problems. All the problems he caused for himself, all the trouble and prison term that he brought on himself. Blames us for it. That's why he's here."

I was on the other side of the wall, waiting, listening, to see what else they would do. The only one doing the talking now was Monica, into her cell phone, telling the police operator to send cops over; they had a break-in. She gave the address. I decided it was time to get out of the area.

Chapter 36

It was going to be a lot tougher now to carry out what I had in store for the bitches. It didn't mean I couldn't pull it off, just that it would be a real task to carry out.

When I looked up, Bruno's car was still sitting there at the curb, Bix Nix crying. Bruno doing his best to calm him down. He was rubbing the back of his neck. Bix was actually crying in the other man's shoulder. Sobbing like a baby. What the hell kind of man was this? All that muscle, major tubesteak; thick neck, Mr. Olympia physique, and he was blubbering like a baby, because he hadn't been able to get it up to shag that bimbo back there.

What was I going to do now? Walk away? Pass up the opportunity to deep-six Grozewski? Here he was. *Right in front of me. I had him.* But if I took care of him, wasted his sorry ass, Bix was a witness. I'd have to take him out, too. And I didn't want to do that. I knew I'd hate myself if I killed the punk. Punk had done nothing to me. Absolutely nothing. In fact, I had him to thank for making it possible for me to lay that blond hottie back there. It was true. If he'd been able to get it up, I would have been fucked. Big time.

What was I going to do? Rollers were on their way. *Rollers.* And I had Bruno sitting in his car no more than thirty feet from me. They had no idea I was behind them, crouching next to a parked car, gun in hand. Waiting. Deciding what to do.

The whole thing made me ill. I didn't want to take out an innocent bystander's life. I didn't. So help me. This was not me.

Would I? Was I going to? What choice did I have?

Anyone reading this is going to say: *Reed killed the guy because he was gay.* Didn't matter that it wasn't true. This is what they would be saying. He killed the guy out of jealousy; because the sissy had a big dick and the looks and body—and Freddie hated that about him, and wasted his ass.

It was a dilemma, in a long life of dilemmas. One after another. Waste Bix Dixon, and have Bruno drive us out to the pre-dug graves; chain him to a tree out there by the shack, bring the two wenches out, then turn them loose, wrists cuffed behind their backs, turn them loose and let them take off. Well, I wouldn't cuff the wenches' wrists behind their backs probably, cuff them, not together, but leave the cuffs on. But in Grozewski's case, cuff his behind his back, and let the fat *tub-of-shit* try to outrun me this way.

Bix was crying still. And Bruno was the comforting Daddy. He had the hots for the young stud with the impressive *chorizo*, but now he was being extra supportive.

Shoot him. Shoot Bix, and get it over with, and hit the road with Grozewski. Do it. Just do it. Time is running out. Rollers are on the way. You have no time to lose. None. Get it over with.

I was scared. Sick to my belly and scared. Because of what I was about to do.

Chapter 37

What I really wanted was to go back in there, grab the rest of them: Monica, Margie, Modi and the dippy blond. Get them all. Take them with. Out to the desert and deal with them out there. Because if I didn't, Monica and Margie would blab about me to the rollers. And if it got out, if my name got mentioned, they'd be after me. There would be nowhere to run after that. A former pig (Grozewski) iced, and how many people all told? Bix, Modi, Margie, Lucy and Monica? How many was that? I was too nervous to count, add 'em up. I had to make my move.

And if I did go in, how was I going to get the bitches to drop their guns? Couldn't be done. Not this way. There had to be something, a move I hadn't thought of, a move that hadn't occurred to me.

Chapter 38

The gate was sliding open, and Monica stepped through, and walked over to Bruno's car, driver's side. She still had that roscoe in her hand, and kept looking around while addressing one annoyed Grozewski.

"You didn't happen to see him? He leapt over the wall back there."

"Who are we talking about?"

"Who did I say?"

"Fred Reed? What makes you think he's even in California?"

"It was him, I tell you."

"Bullshit, Monica! See what you and Margie have done to *him?"* Grozewski was indicating his pal Bix. "He's distraught, so distraught— and for what? You couldn't give him a break. The one person who desperately needs a break. You shot him down without so much as a real chance."

"He couldn't get it up, Bruno. Why lay blame on me and Margie? You saw it. And you also saw Redd Dogg—*Freddie*, rather—jump her bones like a thoroughbred; never having appeared in a porn video in his life. Why? Because he enjoys fucking women. Your friend here—no offense, Bix—is used to shagging men. Nothing the matter with it. We can offer him work in our next all-male epic. Only there is no way he's playing Fred Reed in our mainstream version of what took place there."

"This is too much. You're obsessed with him, you and Margie. Can't seem to get Fred Reed out of your system. Doesn't matter that he's been away, locked up, behind bars all these years. You never heard from him;

he never badgered either of you, but you insist on bringing his name up. Make the film, but stop imagining things. I don't need you to pretend that he's on the premises, simply to cover up the fact that you and Margie were rude to my friend. You broke his heart in there; and owe him an apology."

"Fuck you, Bruno!" Margie had walked up. "That goes for your boyfriend there: Bix!" She held up her middle finger. "Monica is too nice, but I'm not. Here! *Fuck the both of you!* I saw him with my own eyes; and she's not imagining anything! Freddie, the certified *nut-job asshole* is back! To cause us trouble. And if I were you I'd watch it. Keep this in mind: You were just as responsible for sending him up the creek. The three of us had an equal hand in it. You want to pretend it didn't happen, go right ahead. We're taking extra precaution, because we remember what he's like; what he's about! And what he's about is *payback*! That's why he was hiding out in the studio."

"He's been in the house." Monica was getting her two cents in. "*Sniffing around.* Took the Glock that I keep in my purse, changed his mind and left it on the kitchen counter, *after he'd taken the bullets out.* That's not something I imagined or made up. *We're giving you facts, Bruno.* Take heed. Cops are on the way."

"You called Valley PD?" From the way he reacted it sounded like he felt they were wasting their time. They wouldn't answer. "Wouldn't hold my breath."

According to Monica, they were definitely on their way.

"Knowing how they work, you'll be lucky if they get here under two hours."

"We'll wait."

Chapter 39

"It just occurred to me, he never signed a release."

"What are you talking about, Margie?"

"Fred never signed. We can't use the scene we just shot with him unless he signs a release; otherwise we risk getting sued."

"At a time like this, Marge? You're bringing this up? Who cares about a goddamned release, hon? We use it. If he decides to pursue legal action, let him. He hasn't got a pot to piss in. How's he going to retain a lawyer? Besides, all he has to do is come in to get compensated. And we get him to sign when he does—and have him thrown back in jail where he belongs."

Grozewski's cell went off. I couldn't make it out exactly, but it didn't sound pleasant. I was guessing his live-in roomie Percy was pissed because Bruno was spending too much time with Bix Dixon.

"He was tested. Yes, they read him, Percy. Then he did a scene with this *'ingenue.'* Well, tried to. It was a flop." Then: "What am I still doing here? It's a long story that I don't feel like getting into." Bruno stopped talking to do some listening. For a moment. "He took it hard, Percy. Real hard. When am I coming home?" His eyes were on Monica and her roomie. "Are we staying, or are we leaving, ladies?"

Monica and Margie looked at each other.

"He'd like a chance to make a couple of bucks. Main reason we're here. The least you can do to help out; after what he's just been put through. He's flat broke, why Percival and I let him stay with us. Can you please put something together, Monica?"

"Now?"

"I realize it's short notice."

"After all that's happened? You want us to put something together right now? At this hour?"

"Please? Would you consider it? For old time's sake."

Monica sighed, then shook her head. She cursed under her breath.

"We can try. Sure."

Bruno was back on his cell, relaying this info to his partner at the other end.

Chapter 40

I needed to climb back over the wall. About the only option I had at this juncture. If I attempted to hightail it on foot in a quiet residential neighborhood like this where no one walked, I'd get bagged for sure. It would take a while to get to where I'd left my ride parked with Payback in it. Rollers were on their way. Get back on the property, hide out, and wait for the opportunity to make my move.

Grozewski and his protege had stepped out of Bruno's car. He'd given the kid a Kleenex to wipe his eyes with, then a comb, while talking on his cell. Sounded like he was communicating with some of his piggy buds at Valley *Five-0* headquarters.

Monica had walked away, and was waiting by the gate. So had Margie, until she heard what the former piggy was saying to the party on the other end.

"Just what do you think you're doing, you fat fuck?" Margie was the one doing the screaming. Like mother/like daughter. She walked up to his side of the car.

"Calling them off, Marge. We can't have cops coming around when we're getting ready to shoot a gang-bang."

"Who gave you permission? Who gave you the okay? We had our home invaded by a stalker, goddamn you! What is your problem? Are you that fucking dense?"

He looked at Monica, who walked up.

"You want cops coming around now? After what we decided to go ahead with?"

The dick-obsessed former piggy couldn't wait to see his protege get reamed by a gang of thugs with large tools. Didn't give a rat's ass about anything else. He couldn't get into the Idaho spud's crapper, so he'd settle for the next best thing: watch him get drilled by others. Effing lowlife. This was the *bottom-feeder* who sent me up. Made my life a living hell for helping get rid of another *bottom-feeder* named Frank Graham. Go figure. Better yet: don't figure. Anything.

I still needed to get back over that wall, and hide out somewhere. I needed to nail the bitches, nab them, and bury them. Those shallow graves were waiting. Hated to see all that hard work it took to dig the holes go to waste.

"Your call, Monica."

"No one gave you permission to cancel the police. It would only make sense to have them at least write up a report of the incident."

"No need to have them show for that. I'm saying this as a former detective: on the force here, as well as in the Midwest. All you—and Margie—do is drive to the station in the morning and fill out a report. But if you do that, he'll never sign the release. Up to you. It's still not a good idea to have cops stopping by for this. It really isn't. They'll talk to your neighbors. It's negative publicity you don't need at this point. You've had enough of that, don't you think?"

Monica stood there, staring/glaring at him, as did Margie. It looked like they'd had it with this portly loser. It seemed they were finally, at last, seeing him for what he truly was: dipstick idiot of a has-been fat fuck doughnut eater. I could have told them as much. Look what he was doing, just to see the young stud take prick up his rectum and/or see him suck pipe; chug sperm. It made you sick. At least it did me. I hoped I didn't have to see it. If I had to hide out on the property, I hoped it wouldn't have to be back in the studio.

Margie was in his face. "All this, just to get your *jollies*. That's it, isn't

Bruno? You motherfucker. Explains why you and Frank were so close. Explains why he never had any lead left for me when he got home, after spending time with you."

"Now, wait just a minute. No need to be disrespectful here. I thought we were friends."

"With friends like you, who needs vipers?"

I recalled the line. Used by Graham in his tête-à-tête with Rinelle that time, years before. Monica was quick to second what Margie just said. And Margie wasn't done. *"I read you like a book."*

"Cancel, or not?" Grozewski was looking at Monica. "Your call."

"At this point? *What difference does it make?* Freddie's long gone by now."

Chapter 41

I had climbed over the back wall and landed between it and back of the garage. I could hear them out there, in the front yard. I inched my way up alongside the far wall, peeking from behind a hedge. Percy, Bruno's boyfriend was the first to arrive, and the two were arguing. Jealousy. What it came down to. Bruno was spending too much time with the 'hero' from Idaho, and Percy didn't like it. It made him feel insecure, evidently.

"Just trying to help him get back on his feet, Percy."

"Not without me. You don't come over here and pull this shit without me! It was *agreed*! This is *betrayal*, Bruno!"

"Percival —"

"*Don't you Percival me!* It was *agreed*: You would not come over here without me! And you did exactly that! Now you're acting like you don't get why I'm pissed. *Give me a break!*"

"They were all here the whole time! Nothing 'sleazy' took place! Monica, Margie, Monica's son and that new girl: Lucy Ice, I believe her stage name is. All here. So why am I being chastised, Percy? It's uncalled for—and I refuse to take blame for something I'm not guilty of."

"This isn't the first time you've pulled this kind of shit, Bruno!" His partner was screeching. "Where is the *honesty*? *Trust!* This was supposed to be a *monogamous union* here!"

"It is."

"I don't like it. Furthermore, I refuse to take it."

"So you're willing to toss the relationship over a perceived slight, that it? You image a wrong was committed, and that's it? Flush the relationship away? Makes no sense. To flush away, what—8, almost 9 years? Why?"

"Because you can't be trusted!"

The other cocks-for-hire were showing up, pulling up in fancy wheels: Jeeps, Vettes, Benzos and what-not. One or two, of course, drove up in absolute junkers. Most of the bucks they made went up the ol' nose. Both Monica and Margie decided enough was enough of the sniping duo. Monica was the first to put her foot down.

"This bickering needs to stop. And I mean right now."

"She's right." Margie couldn't wait to get in the fray, as usual. So much of the way she acted and the loud way she had of talking reminded me of her dead ho mamma. Rinelle. "Take it home; take it wherever you want, but not here. Not now or anytime, as a matter of fact. We've got work to do—and a positive atmosphere *is-a-must*, lest we give the wrong impression to the talent."

The bickering gay men couldn't/wouldn't stop.

"*Enough!* You're not putting the director on the spot. Shut-up, or get banned—for good. I mean it. There is work to be done. Monica needs to focus on that, and not your bullshit bickering."

"What bullshit?" Was it Percival? It was Percival. "It's not *'bullshit.'* This is my life! I've taken as much as I can off this two-faced fag!"

"Okay." Margie pointed a finger at him. "Get in your car and drive off. Leave. *You're gone.*"

"Wait —"

She held up her cell. "Percy, leave—or we call *Five-0. Now.* We've had it up to here."

Bruno's boyfriend cursed under his breath, got in his car, and pulled out.

The talent, five studs: white and black, climbed out of their vehicles. Couple of them dressed in suits, others casual: in jeans, shorts, etc. Bruno's eyes lit up. He went around glad-handing those he was familiar with, then he did the same bit with those he was *not* familiar with.

Chapter 42

I couldn't stick around. No matter how hard I tried to convince myself that I needed to. As curious as I was to see how many of these fucks would end up drinking the antifreeze, it just was not reason enough. My idea of a group-grope and/or gang-bang would have been: Monica, Margie and Lucy Ice and me. Or, if possible, a couple of other good-looking built wenches with tight *culos* and dripping wet twats, and not a bunch of low-life bottom-feeding Porn Valley mooks reaming and creaming all over a healthy looking and naive kid like Bix Dixon.

The only alternative to finding out who drank what, would be to return to Pinocchio's the next day and see who shows up. There was also that other incentive: money owed to me for the decent tongue job I laid on Lucy Ice. Sure. Why not? Money always talked. There were always ways to spend it. Didn't matter that you had a death wish and intended to check out. And who knew what Monica and Margie planned on doing with the scene? Make it part of some kind of anthology. Call it: *Daddy Knows Best.* Or: *Daddy Taught Me the Ins & Outs of Shagging.*

I didn't care what they named it or what they did with it. All I knew: If they wanted my autograph, they'd have to fork over some decent bread. And what if after I signed and got paid, Monica and Margie decided to press charges? Report my breaking into their place? I'd get what for that? Deny it? I could. It would be the two of them, against one of me. I'd lose. Would I get jail time for it?

No. There is the video footage that would 'prove' I'd gone in with permission. Even Grozewski had been under the impression the whole thing had been set up beforehand by Monica and her partner as backup, in case his boy Bix failed to deliver the groceries.

So what did I have to fear? Instead, I stood to gain: with the money I'd be able to buy a few more things, as well as food for Payback, and then give what remained of the money to someone to take care of him after I was gone. I scaled the wall and got out of there.

Chapter 43

It was a good thing, too, because when I got back to the van it was obvious my four-legged pal was eager to go for a walk. I grabbed the box of dog biscuit treats and off we went for a stroll in the ritzy neighborhood. It didn't take him long to go. We must've been in front of some rich showbiz mook's house when Payback decided to take a dump. It filled me with great joy to watch him drop a big load on the perfectly manicured lawn. Payback was in no hurry, either. It did not take long for some ancient fuck with uncombed, long hair, a reject from the 60s hippie era, in a bathrobe and slippers to come rushing out, waving his index finger, cursing at us. I looked up, calm as could be. So was Payback, releasing log after log. The pissed Tinseltown loon came on. I held my middle finger up, knowing it would only intensify his rage. Then when he got close enough, I drew my piece. That stopped him cold. His arms went up. Rich and spoiled, he still had gall to bitch, though. Fucking scumbag hippie must've been on a cocaine high. Had the red nostrils and sniffles.

"You got no idea how much it costs to keep this lawn looking like this. Dog urine destroys grass. Property value goes down when there's dog shit around."

"Is that so?"

"I'm in real estate. I'm telling you. Dog waste depreciates property. It's tough enough to keep it off the grounds as it is."

"I can think of one way to keep it off, asshole: *make you eat it*. If you're not back inside that over-priced cribby of yours by the count of three, that's exactly what you'll be doing: *ingesting* my dog's *turds*."

I started counting. Suddenly something made me stop. There was what appeared to be a joint stuck between a couple of his fingers, left hand.

"That a bong?"

"Cocoa puff."

He started to explain.

"Shut the fuck up."

I took a good hit, and commenced the countdown.

". . . One thousand one . . . one thousand two . . . one thousand . . ."

He was inside and slamming his door shut. I finished the bong, unzipped, and watered his grass like a 'Russian race horse.' What we used to say—as young punks—back in the Midwest whenever we had to take a leak: *"I gotta piss like a Russian race horse."*

Payback responded with his final opinion on the matter: one last log, and was ready to continue our stroll. I gave him a couple of dog biscuit treats, and we resumed our adventure through this high-toned hood.

Chapter 44

Yep. They were there the following night. Chipper. Smiling. Well, with the exception of Bruno's boyfriend. He especially didn't seem to be happy that Bix was sitting next to his soulmate Grozewski. I only refer to Bruno as being his roomie's 'soulmate' because that's the word his roomie kept using. Soulmate.

"I thought we were *soulmates*, Bruno."

"We remain so, Percy, honey."

Monica was looking at me, while I walked from table to table tossing plates into the plastic tub.

"Surprised to see you here. I must confess, Fred."

"Why is that?"

"Because of what took place last night."

"Exactly why I'm here. Somebody owes me a good chunk of cash. For services rendered."

She pulled out a contract, then waved a check. I went over to take a glance at the amount.

"You're joking."

"Three hundred is a fair amount for that scene."

"Twice that would be closer to what I had in mind."

Both Marge and Monica appeared to be taken aback.

"You wouldn't want to screw an old friend."

"We could've filed a report, but never did."

"Only because you liked the scene so much and needed me to sign on the dotted line, Monica."

Neither of the wenches said anything.

"Pay me what I'm worth, and we'll do a few more—and you've got yourself a series: older, handsome gent/younger wench hottie. Call it what you like, but I thought something along the lines of: *Daddy Was My First*, or else, call it: *Seduced by Uncle Sly*."

"Five hundred." Monica's counter offer. She had come a long way since I knew her back in the day when she was a lowly secretary to Sonny Sheldon.

I stuck with six. Six seemed like a nice round number to stick with. I'd been a sucker too often in the past. I needed money. Dog food wasn't free, and neither was gasoline—and where I intended to take them was way the fuck out in the sticks, away from the city, miles and miles away. Besides, who was going to look after Payback? I'd talked to someone out there, a desert rat living in an RV who was willing to take him on after I was gone. I'd give the man what was left of the money for the dog's upkeep. Seemed like the right thing to do.

I kept moving about, performing my bussing duties. If I didn't get what I wanted, they didn't get my John Hancock. That simple. She waved a new check around. I insisted on cash. They scraped it together. This time I signed the release.

Chapter 45

"She'd like to do another scene with you." Monica was intent on talking some more shit, no doubt.

"Lucy. She's in love with you. Well, your tongue, anyway. You make love with such zeal. It was memorable for her."

"And for me. Only because I'd gone years without."

"What do you say?"

"If you and Margie joined in. For old time's sake." Why I'd said it I couldn't tell. Must have been half-joking. Better yet, fucking with them. To see what the dykes would come back with.

"We don't fuck males." It was the big mouth. Margie. Couldn't wait. Her loathing of the male runneth over. "Especially jerks named *Alf Reed*."

She knew I didn't like being called Alf. I let that part go.

"Venom so thick you could cut it with a knife."

"Venom? *Venom?* Fuck you. You came back to disrupt our lives. Only reason you're not back in jail is because you're good at eating pussy; about the only thing you're good for. It saved your ass. You made some decent money for getting that young babe off. You're offered even more money for an opportunity to turn your life around and ditch this nothing shit job you got here; and what's your response? How do you react? Like the typical asshole we've always known you to be. Born loser. I can see this is a waste. Next time you break into our place, you're going down, fucker. You're effing toast. You don't set foot on our property unless we give you permission; unless you're invited! Get it, *chump*?"

"The '*chump*' gets it. I'd also like to point out that you're sending mixed messages. She wants me for another scene, and you want to send me back to Q., as if I didn't do enough time; as if I hadn't paid enough dues."

Margie was about to say something else. Monica placed her hand over hers, to calm her down.

"Margie, if your goal is to get me shit-canned, you're doing a pretty damned good job of it."

"You'll get shit-canned with or without our help."

"Will you do another scene with Lucy Ice?"

"Maybe. Toss in another hottie like her, someone stacked, with a great ass—and I just might consider it. For the right price."

I really was not interested in pursuing porn as a career. The only thing I was interested in was seeing the three '*triple-threats*' drop down into the graves that waited for them in the desert.

But if a scene, the possibility of another scene taking place on their property presented itself, and it seemed to be . . . I had a thought, well, the notion had actually occurred the night before, when I saw Monica's kid pull up in that fancy van: the perfect vehicle to carry the three out to the holes: Margie, Monica and Bruno. (Only because Modi's van was much nicer and had a good strong engine in it, as opposed to what was under the hood of my junker.) But yes, his van had made me think along those lines: knock them out, or wait until they consumed some of that antifreeze, carry them inside his van, and drive out. But then what about Modi? And whoever else happened to be there: what would I do about them? Take care of them somehow?

I knew Modi would be there; if Lucy was there, so would Modi be, as he appeared to be pimping the chick. Should it happen this way, what about Grozewski? What would I do there? I'd have to drive out to his place, knock his ass out, and carry him inside the van. This piggy weighed plenty. There had to be an easier way. *There had to be.*

Figure out how to get him back to Monica and Margie's studio. And the only way to do that, would be to have a reason for Bix to show. If Bix was there, it was almost guaranteed that so would be the former roller.

Chapter 46

The wine connoisseurs were drinking their wine and I wondered when the effect would take place, or would it be like before? Nada.

I was at the far end of the diner when I caught my first sign out of the corner of my eye that something was not right with our happy and ambitious Hollywood players. Monica was the first: stomach cramps. Nausea. It was beautiful to see. She had her arms crossed across her lower belly. Clutching that part. Not unlike Frank Graham whenever he took a sip of that 'healthy' raspberry iced tea from that thermos years before, not unlike yours truly that time I had my first and only sip upon Graham's insistence. Margie took notice and wondered what was up.

"What's the matter, sweetie?"

Monica appeared to be in a trance, not saying anything, just staring straight ahead. Not blinking even. I watched her wince; eyes closed.

"Oh God."

A sigh. One of discomfort. Clearly. Margie proceeded to pat her on the shoulder. Monica brushed her hand off, stood up and staggered to the john in a kind of hurry. Moments later one of the most beautiful sounds I ever heard was so loud that it hit all of us in the dining area.

Both Margie and Grozewski had a concerned look on their mugs. Yeah. Worry. I didn't recall them having these looks and/or expressions on their effing kissers when the judge threw the book at me. Oh no. Nothing remotely close to it. In fact, what I saw was smugness. Yessiree, Bobby. They were smug and pleased.

I wondered who would be next? I didn't have to wonder for long: because Margie was vomiting on the floor. Making grunts and pleading, once again, to a god who never existed, and vomiting her guts out.

If Monica's little turn of events was a joy to witness, this was better. Oh, this was way better. The loud mouth was making all kinds of loud noises and gasps. You'd have thought the over-the-hill shrew was dying. When in fact, there was no way. Not here; not now. Because I hadn't poured enough of that antifreeze into the bottle. Nope. Didn't want them to croak here. Merely wished to see them suffer a bit. Call it the *pre-death preview. Trailer.* Of things to come. They were in the film and tv business. Wasn't that what they called those things? Take a quick gander of features to come.

She rose, with Bruno's help, needing to get her to the john, only Bruno wasn't going anywhere himself, because he released a series of farts, and started not only vomiting, but was shitting his pants. Antifreeze had given him the runs. *Deja vu.* Where had I seen this before?

Oh, this was too beautiful for words. If only I could have had a video camera right now for this. Surely, I would have taped it—for posterity's sake.

Margie, bent over, staggered to the ladies' room. And Bruno? He couldn't budge, the diarrhea continued to run down his trousers. And his heartbroken boyfriend? Pleased as punch. So happy and thrilled. The look on his face saying: *You had it coming to you, two-timing faggot!*

"Shut up, Percy."

"I never said a word, honey."

"Just shut-up!"

Bruno didn't want to hear it, whatever it was. I watched him leap from the table and hurry to the men's room, farting every agonizing step of the way.

Chapter 47

The manager of the place, Aldo Picasso, finally came out to the dining area. I made like I was busy; and, frankly, I was: dirty plates and silverware needed to be collected and dumped in the plastic tub on my shoulder.

"What's happened here?"

Bix, the teetotaler, was shrugging. Percival could not give up that grin no matter how hard he tried. He shook his head like he gave a damn, but failed there as well.

"Something they ate. Or drank. They're in the john, puking their guts out. Bruno soiled himself. What a sorry state of affairs."

Aldo was speechless. What did this mean? Lawsuit? If not a lawsuit, it still meant plenty of trouble for Pinocchio's.

He walked over to me.

"Redd Dogg, can you tell me what's going on?"

Instead of going with his typical belligerent tone, he was using a hushed approach. Sounded almost human. It threw me momentarily.

"They doing drugs? Toot? That's it isn't it, Redd Dogg? Did you see them *snorting*? You can level with me."

I looked at him without saying a word.

"I'm talking to you, *Redd Dogg*. You give them drugs? That's it, isn't it? Didn't matter that you risked my job. I got a family, asshole. That don't mean shit to you."

"I didn't see anyone abusing illegal substances, Mr. Picasso. Besides, I was busy tending to my duties here: cleaning up, picking up plates."

"What'd they have to drink?"

"I don't know, sir. I never served them anything. That's not my job. That's the servers' job. I keep my nose out of other peoples' affairs."

"Bullshit. *Fucking transient.* Trouble-making *mook.* Should fire you on the spot. Got this feeling you're behind this somehow."

I said nothing.

"Only reason you're not fired is because I don't have all the facts. Once I put it all together, you're out of here, buddy. Like that other jerk I canned. Got that *Redd Dogg?* You're gone. Same as Henry. Buncha losers."

"Do what you gotta, Mr. Picasso."

I walked away with the full tub of dirty china and utensils. I heard him curse under his breath, then walk over to where the restrooms were and started calling their names in quick succession. Only nobody was answering.

Chapter 48

Good, I thought. Maybe the mothers are dead. All three of them. Save me the trouble of the rest of it. Sure, I'd feel short-changed, cheated—but what the fuck?

Only the assholes weren't dead, on account we could hear all three vomiting through the closed doors of the restrooms.

He knocked on the women's door. And I heard Margie scream. "Don't come in here, motherfucker! You got a lawsuit on your hands!"

"Lawsuit?"

"Food poisoning and tainted wine! You're in deep shit, mister! You're effed. Big time!"

Aldo said nothing. Sighed, then moved over to the men's room door. Went in. Bruno could be heard shitting up a storm. He had a super bad case of the runs. Sounded something like an elephant in there taking a violent and painful dump.

Oh, it was worth it. Wished I could stand beside them and watch and chuckle my ass off. Only I was glad that it wasn't possible. Bruno smelled up the joint. Bad. It was tough to take.

Aldo closed the door. Stepped away. Took a few steps toward the kitchen in back and froze, just froze, glaring at me. I pretended like I didn't notice, like I had my mind on work. Only I think he was smart enough to detect/pick up the smirk on my face. Not that I'm in the habit of smirking, or having anything like a smug look on, but this time, *this one time*, I believe I was the proud owner of both.

He pointed his index finger at me, and held it. I mean he just held it like that—without uttering so much as a syllable. Then just as suddenly, continued on to the kitchen.

Chapter 49

Did I actually care? Did I? I'll tell you how much I cared. I felt like dropping the tub full of dishes and forks and spoons and knives, instead I lowered it onto one of the tables, untied my apron, and casually unlocked the front door. That's when I stopped, and retraced my steps. I lifted that tub and spun with it, and watched all those plates and chunks of food and forks and knives and glasses go flying all over the floor and tables. I took my time walking back to the front door. I heard Aldo emerge from the kitchen.

"*What the fuck, schmuck?*"

My middle finger shot straight up, and I waved it around; then my other finger went up, and I waved them both—with a nice grin on my face to accompany the gestures.

"Kindly choke on excreta, punk, and expire."

"*You cocksucker. Redd Dogg.*"

He moved toward me. In a real hurry like. Good, I thought. I reached for my shoulder rig, timing it. By the time he got to me the business end of my .357 Magnum was up against the hair in his nostrils. Pretty much ended his mobility.

"Now what, dick snot? Who you gonna *blow* to get out of this fix? *Who you gonna call?* Kojak? Go ahead, *punk*. Tell 'em I pitched your plates all over your grimy floor—on account your abuse was hard to take."

He kept his mouth shut. Scared shitless. Hell, I thought he might do a Bruno Grozewski number and take a dump in his panties. Only he didn't.

I stepped outside. Made it toward my ride. Oooh. If you've ever walked away from a soul-sapping shit job, you would know exactly how this felt.

Chapter 50

I got in that rattling junk heap of a van, affixed the muzzle to Payback's snout, politely requested that he keep his growling down to a minimum, and took it around to the front. Not near the entrance, but not so far away that I wouldn't be able to see who drove up to get the vomiting vermin.

I figured an ambulance would draw too much attention and result in negative publicity and Aldo would call a cab. And the cabbies I knew, had known, didn't like cleaning up vomit in the backseat. All I had to do was wait and see what happened.

A Valley cab eventually pulled up forty minutes later. Cabs around here took their time. And the Three Musketeers limped out, moaning and groaning, threatening to sue Pinocchio's. I reached for a camcorder and did my Bertolucci bit.

Bruno was still farting, you could easily hear it even from where I sat parked and watched the whole pathetic situation. Was there a taxi driver alive who would let a guy with stained pants get in his cab and soil the interior and ruin his night for him? Doubtful.

And then Margie, the biggest mouth in Porn Valley, had to pause to expel some more bile. She wiped with the back of her hand, cursing and screaming and wanting to know why there was no ambulance.

"He begged us not to . . ."

Monica's explanation was feeble, between wiping tears and snot from her face.

"Who the fuck is *'he'*, Monica?"

"Aldo. It would look bad."

"*Fuck Aldo! We* look bad! There must've been something in that lasagna, or the salad, or Caesar Dressing."

"The wine."

It was Grozewski's turn to groan. Tripped on his own feet. Bix came up from behind to hold him up.

Well, my cinema geniuses got as far as the cab's rear door, one of whom grabbed the door handle—only it wouldn't open. They tried again. Margie cursed, and demanded that the cabbie unlock it.

The driver stuck his head out through the rolled down passenger window.

"I don't take drunks. You peeps are dunk. And that gentleman there? Looks like he shit his pants."

"*You're not taking us?*" Margie stayed with the incredulous tone. Not that it got her anywhere. "We just want to get home. *You're refusing to take us?*"

"There's a big tip in it for you."

"Ain't a tip big enough to get me to take you, sir."

On that, the cabbie pulled away. Margie was cursing up a storm, like the Margie of old—and flipped him the bird. This was music to my ears. Scene gave me a certain satisfaction inside. Dirtbags. Self-centered, disgusting sacks of horse dung. I didn't blame the cabbie; I couldn't. I would've done the same, I thought, as I turned the key in the ignition and pulled up. I was still shooting video.

Chapter 51

"Get in, Margie."

"A human being. At last. Endangered species." She must not have recognized my voice right away, from what I gathered as a result of what I heard next.

"Is that you, Modigliani? *Modi?*"

The van did look enough like his. It was dark out. It was late.

"Sight for sore eyes." What she thought. Until she opened the passenger door, and then her expression changed. I lowered the camcorder.

"I'm here to help. Reconsidered your offer. You're right: Chance of a lifetime. Up to you, Margie."

She stayed put. I got out. Went around and slid the side door open for the others.

Bruno staggered in and plopped down on the mattress, followed by Monica. Margie remained standing. Undecided. I reached for the open passenger door and opened it wider in an effort to help her decide.

She finally went for it. Climbed in. I closed her door. Even managed a smile while doing it. Bix slid the side door closed without climbing in himself. I guess he'd had enough of it: the puke, stench, screaming and cursing. For all of his prowess in the sack, as a gay stud, he was a mild-mannered type—and who could blame him? In fact, I was okay with Mr. Bix Dixon not going along. It meant one less human to have to deal with. It meant less worry. It also meant one less life I'd have to take.

I returned to the driver's seat. Payback handled himself beautifully. Knew to maintain when he was ordered to. The muzzle helped, no doubt.

I was looking at Margie.

"Be happy, don't worry."

"How about if you zip it and drive, *jag-off*?"

Jag-off was the Midwest version of jerk-off. Not that it mattered. Meant the same thing.

"Get us the fuck out of here."

"Yes." It was Monica. "Please." Polite to the very last. Cold-blooded, heartless, but always polite. Even when she was being spanked and having her backside drilled by a massive dildo. Polite through and through.

I turned my head to see how the two in the back were doing. Out. Snoring and moaning. Margie still awake, bitching and cursing, but her eyes were open. No problem. I'd take care of her in a moment. I had plans.

I got us out of there.

Chapter 52

Margie was having a tough time keeping her eyes open.

"Are we home yet?" Inquiry came from the back. Sounded like Monica.

Bruno was muttering Bix's name. Something about being in lust with him. "It's not love, Bix. It can't be. I'm hurting Percy. I can't betray Percy. I can't, Bix."

"We there, Margie?"

"No, we aren't. Because we seem to be going the wrong way, taking a route that makes no sense."

"What did you say?"

Monica was aching, and she had the dry heaves. She'd vomited so much back at Pinocchio's that there didn't seem to be anything left to puke.

"I said we are going the wrong way, Monica." Margie was looking at me. "What's up with that, *Alf?* Where the fuck are you taking us—in this serial killer van? This is the kind of van a serial killer would own."

She leaned out the open window and threw up. Wiped with the back of her sleeve, and kept looking at me. I had the camcorder going. Had it down at waist level and was shooting footage of her. Margie noticed and it seemed to increase her ire.

"Are you taping this? Goddamn you!"

My response was to grin.

"Stop this fucking *serial killer* van and let me out."

"Sure, Margie. No problem."

I stopped the van, reached under my seat for the rubber mallet, got out, and walked to her side. I opened the passenger door, all the while shooting footy. It didn't take much; didn't take long, but I drove that hammer right into her jaw. It was fast, like lightning quick, and she slumped back against the seat.

"I hate, *hate* serial killers. And dislike being compared to them."

That really stung. Being called a shit-bird serial whacko. In fact, if I had the time, if I could ever make it happen, I'd go after them myself. Go on a world-wide hunt for serial turds. But I was too old for it. Time was running out. I had a mission to accomplish, a job to do. My hands were tied.

I stowed the camcorder. Dug into the pocket of my cargo pants and fished out a pair of cuffs. I drew her arms behind her, and cuffed her wrists.

"Serial killers are *punks, pedophiles, rapos. That's not me*. I don't molest kids, I don't rape bitches. I don't harm animals. I play *get back. Payback. Get even. Steven.*"

"Hey." Sounded like Bruno moaning. "What's going on?"

I closed Margie's door. Slid open the side door, and stood there. Stench was incredibly bad. Vomit and waste.

"I'll tell you what's going on. You ruined my van, is what."

I climbed in, bashed him in the face, twice, then gave Monica a solid one across her jaw. I cuffed their wrists behind their back, climbed down, slid the side door closed. I climbed in the driver's seat. Margie was moaning. In and out of it. Face was bleeding. Tears and snot and blood oozed down that loud snout of hers, that was no longer cursing and/or threatening. The other two did their share of moaning as well: sounds of pain and discomfort. I think those cuffs may have been clamped on a bit tight.

Pre-dug graves waited out there for us.

Chapter 53

Margie continued to moan and shake her head, mumbling, cursing and threatening. The only thing that kept me from driving that mallet into her big mouth again was the fact I needed her to have enough strength and stamina for later on and the plans I had for her. So I let her moan; I let all three moan and plead and beg to be un-cuffed.

"Sure."

I pulled up to the curb about a third of a block from a mini-mart. I reached inside the glove compartment for the roll of duct tape. Tore off a strip and taped Margie's yap shut. Then I tore off a couple more. Took care of her pals.

I draped one of the worn blankets over Margie, urged her to stay down in the seat, and pulled into the minimart parking lot, parking in the poorly-lighted right side of the building that was devoid of cars. The few cars in evidence were parked in front of the store.

I went in. This called for a celebration of sorts: beer, cigar, something to eat. Burger or hot dog. What I ingested no longer mattered. Junk food? In a world that was crawling with *junk humans*? Bring it on. What difference did it make what you consumed and/or exposed your system to?

No difference.

Besides, everything was full of chemicals. GMOs. Corporations were committing murder on a grand and massive scale. And got away with it. *Mental illness, Alzheimer's, cancer.* All for *profit*. That's how it worked. You killed one human or two, you went to jail. You killed thousands, no sweat. Because it came down to the reason—and *murder for profit* was the best and most excusable reason of all. And yes; there's that other one. Called *war*.

I added potato chips to the lot, peanuts, box of ginger snaps. Paid for the items, and returned to the van. A transient approached me. White dude in his 30s. Slimy, grimy and bearded. Strung out, no doubt. Asking for 'spare change.' He smelled as bad as Bruno and the two bitches.

"Sure, homey."

I gave him two singles. He was grateful. He stood there looking at me, while scratching his crotch.

"Don't I know you from somewhere? You ever do time?"

"Did time with your mama."

"My mama's a ho."

"Welcome to the club, bro."

I got in, yanked the strip of tape off Monica's mug, then did the same for the former law enforcement flunky. I pulled back the part of the blanket that had been over Margie's face, but did not remove the duct tape. I didn't want to have to hear her utter a single syllable for a while. Then I pulled out. We had a long drive ahead of us.

Chapter 54

I took a bite of the hot dog, stuck a few chips in my mouth. I looked at Margie. Coming to, her eyes doing the eyelid batting number: *I can't believe the nightmare I'm stuck in.*

"Believe it."

Then I asked if she was hungry. Not sure why. Maybe just to fuck with her. I got no answer.

"S'matter? Cat got your tongue?"

She wasn't talking. Shook her head, but didn't say a word, or tried to— or maybe she did. The gag made it tough.

"Even a ball-buster like you deserves a last meal."

My eyes were on her crotch and the urine stain there. Margie had pissed her jeans. Healthy ass, domineering Margie had wet herself.

Just as well. The piggy had shit his pants, one bitch was covered in puke, and this one had wet herself and soiled the seat. Did it matter? Make any difference? Nope. None of it. I'd been headed this way my whole life. Sealed fate. From the day I crawled out of my mama's contaminated womb. Sure, I'd tried to walk that straight and narrow. I did. Did my best. Only it wasn't in the cards. Wasn't meant to be. It took a bit of luck to have any kind of happiness, things to go your way. I just didn't have it. I used to be bummed about it. It used to frustrate me, make me angry; caused me so much anxiety. But now? I accept it. None of it matters anyway. Not much made any difference.

I kept the beer inside the sack, out of sight, in case I got stopped. And then it occurred to me: if I got pulled over by the rollers it didn't make sense to have a bloody-faced Margie G. sitting in the front with me like this.

I stopped the van, grabbed her by the collar and dragged her in the back and dropped her on top of her pals, where excreta belonged. All three: slime. Not even human, as far as I was concerned. They'd taken great joy in seeing me suffer. I remembered all of it, as if it happened yesterday. Every smirk and dirty look. I was worthless. Not even human. Well, this is what I felt toward them now: nothing. I was looking at a pile of dog shit. And they would be treated as such. The only thing that kept me from smashing their skulls in was that I wanted to see them suffer. I needed to stretch their suffering out for as long as possible.

Spiteful? Who? Me? No shit. For years I was in denial about that. Face it. Admit it. I was one spiteful motherfucker. I never forget a slight; I never forget having been dissed, offended, put down and swept aside—especially after I'd been kind.

Her cell went off; then a moment later so did Monica's. The first made me jump, the other made the hair on the back of my neck stand straight up. I was getting rattled. Just a bit. Fear my plans would go awry. That was it. Mainly. Made my guts get tight inside. I liberated the aging bombshells of their phones. Considered relieving Bruno of his, but the former oinker smelled so bad I thought I'd put it off until I had no choice. I made it back to my seat, and drove.

Chapter 55

Adrenalin was up there, way up there. Talk about rush. I had it. Natural high. Better than a beer buzz and/or toot, Ex or reefer. I just had to remember to keep checking my mirrors. Had to remember that Percy had been back there at the pasta joint. Also needed to remember that Margie had initially thought it was Modi pulling up when I drove up in the van. My conclusion? Somebody must have called him from inside Pinocchio's before they came out.

Maybe, too, I was imagining things. Nerves. It felt real good to be finally doing it, but the fear of being stopped or having someone interfere with my plans before I could finish the project I'd spent years dreaming of and planning could be yanked right from under me. So close; so damned close—only to have it cancelled by some unforeseeable entity . . . like pigs in a squad car, or . . . who knew?

I had to slow down. Watch my driving. Play the law-abiding, conscientious citizen. That was me. Mr. Reed. Three vics in his van. On the way to the killing fields of Joshua Tree. Where the desert sand will run bright crimson with human blood.

The moaning and farting went on back there. The wenches were moaning, Bruno was the one doing the other. As usual. The former piggy had a gas problem. I rolled my window down; then I reached over and rolled the other one down at the next red light.

Chapter 56

One of the cell phones went off in the right pocket of my cargo pants. Now I couldn't remember which was which: whether Margie's was in that pocket, or if it was in the other pocket. On top of that, I had a new dilemma on my hands. Who could be calling? Some porn actor friend of theirs? A crew person looking for work? Pinocchio's? Aldo fearing a lawsuit was on the way? What was I going to do? Answer? Or not answer?

I let it go. The hell with it. If they were desperate to get in touch they'd call again. I did reach inside and fished the cell out. Modigliani. He'd hung up, with a message. He'd also texted a few words:

Where are you? Why did you leave in that other van? Call me back. Modi.

Had me wondering if Aldo might've caught the number on my rear plate.

It was then Bruno's cell went off. Percy was calling, no doubt, wondering what was going on. I let it ring. I'd hoped for a cleaner escape/get away with my vics than this. But what were you going to do? When did things ever go one hundred percent for anybody? When? Like never—that's when. Especially not with a place full of flotsam like this one was. Porn Valley was hopeless, and I was just another hopeless case.

I'd have to remember to get Grozewski's cell. Stench or no stench. I happened to look back just then, and the fuck had the cell in his hand. He'd somehow been able to reach inside his pocket, even with his wrists cuffed that way; he'd been able to reach inside and get his hands on the cell phone, and Monica was attempting to text with her nose.

Son of bitch.

I pulled over. Got back there, kicked the phone away from them and backhanded the fuck across the side of his face.

"You think I'm playing some kind of game here, porky? That it?"

I looked down at Monica. There was fear in her eyes. No way to hide it. She feared me. At long last. And it was plain enough to understand and get and see: She knew; I mean the ho knew what she'd done to me, put me through, her and cunt Margie.

"You're afraid huh? That's good; that's real good, Monica. You not only shredded my heart, but thoroughly enjoyed my suffering. You were the Judas, if there is such a thing as a female Judas; responsible for my crucifixion. I was crucified—for something most men and women get away with with a slap on the wrist. I was wrong, I admit it; I betrayed you. But it was also nothing more than a shag, sex; what I'd been guilty of, and hadn't deserved what I was given. Humans err; we make mistakes; all of us—except you and Margie and this *shit bag* over here. All of us are flawed, except the three of you."

I kicked her in the face, hard. Watched her head bounce against the other bitch. I knelt down, grabbed Margie by her hair, then grabbed Monica by hers—and banged their faces together. Watched the blood ooze from their noses and mouths.

"Want to talk about wrath? *Hell hath no wrath like a woman scorned?* That it? Is that how that goes? Hell has no wrath . . ."

I looked at the former pig. Gave him a kick in the belly that resulted in more flatulence escaping his big ass. While fatso was farting I was searching for his cell phone that had gone flying off somewhere in the back a moment earlier. Finally found it inside the plastic bucket I'd used to wash the van with and/or change the oil from time to time. I sledged the cell with the mallet and tossed the bits outside.

"Motherfuckers."

I returned to the steering wheel. Pulled away from the curb.

Chapter 57

Go home, was my text to Modi. *Sleep tight.*

Mom, Where—Are—You?

I was tempted, so tempted to respond with: I'm tied up at the moment. Love, Mommy. And it took a lot not to.

I drove on through the night. Lightning flashed off in the distance. Thunder roiled. Rain was imminent. I couldn't tell how much or how hard, but it was on the way. I actually wished it wouldn't rain too much, on account it would be tougher to carry out what I had planned. I didn't want to have to track after the bitches in mud, having to wear heavy boots and parka.

It was a thin drizzle for starters, and who knew, maybe it would continue on this way. Well, you dealt with things in life, didn't you? You just dealt with it. I'd been through far worse; I'd been through plenty.

Chapter 58

Dawn was breaking by the time we reached the area. Rain had eased up way back, miles back there. Joshua Tree was barren, for the most part. I got out to relieve myself. Made it possible for the ladies to do the same. Gave them their privacy. So you see, I was not so far gone.

I had the cam going again, wanting to record the next step: drive over to the first grave. Phase was valid enough. I parked the van right beside it, so that once I slid the side door open, all I had to do was grab Grozewski by the belt buckle and heave him out. And this I did, and the former roller rolled right into the muddy grave, landing on his back. Ah, he looked a mess, but those eyes were wide open and he was looking up at me.

"Know what, Bruno? This just occurred to me. Not exactly sure where it comes from, but your first name should've been Bondo. *Bondo* Grozewski. They should have named you *Bondo*. Missed an opportunity there. I prefer Bondo over Bruno any day of the week."

He was still lying on his back, eyes open wide. Huffing; straining to speak through aching teeth.

"Let's hear it, *Bondo*. The usual. How wrong I am to do this."

"You can't. I did what was expected of me. I had a job. You took a friend's life."

"Can't tell the truth . . . even at this late stage, *Bondo?* You're hopeless. Your whole life a waste—something like mine. There is no other way this could end. You fucking die. It's *karma*. I've considered all other possibilities. And all of them come up short, in my estimation."

"Percival . . ."

"What about him?"

"This will destroy him when he discovers that I'm gone. Missing. No body. Nothing to bury, or any way to say good-bye. My kids; my kids should know . . ."

"The plan is to leave certain details in the confession I've been hard at work on; where your bodies can be found."

"Why not just shoot me?"

"Want to give you a chance."

"Burying me alive is giving me a chance?"

"Crawl out. Claw your way to freedom. If you manage, you're a far better man than I figured."

"Un-cuff me. Give me a real chance. Take the cuffs off, Reed. *Take them off.*"

I couldn't see myself doing that. I did un-cuff one wrist, had him place both his hands on his belly and clamped the cuff back on. He claimed he was dying of thirst. I placed a jug of water a few feet from the grave. Suggested it would be there when he crawled out, if he managed to crawl out.

"I'll even leave one of the shovels behind, should a bobcat appear, or a gila monster—to defend yourself with."

"Nice."

"Nicer than the three of you were to me."

I then dropped one end of a three-foot-long hose within easy reach of his mouth, and suggested he suck on it for air, then I un-cuffed the ladies in order to put them to work. Retrieved a shovel from the tool box in the van, detached the entrenching tool from my pack and let them go to it, while the cam recorded it.

They shoveled the dirt in. Some of it mud-like from the rain earlier, the top layer anyway. As weak and as sore as they were, they stayed with it. They were fairly good at taking direction: scooped a full shovel, held it over his face, turned it, while I watched the dirt drop down on his eyes, mouth and nose. I had to remind them that the other end of the hose needed to be unencumbered and poking out, so that the former piggy could take in air—once he was able to get his mouth on his end down there. They did that. Stayed with it, rotating. While the one poured the dirt over him, the other was digging her shovel into the mound beside the grave. Like clockwork.

Eventually I wouldn't be able to see that dirty effing mug, nor be able to smell the stench of him. Stench of a smelly pig. When the grave was full, I had them pat the flat ends of their shovels over it. From one end to the other. Now, this was still fairly loose dirt, and all he had to do was suck in air through the hose, then start clawing and scratching his way with his hands, and moving his head, jerking it—and he had a chance to crawl out. Slim; still a chance. Better than what I'd been given by them. Up to him. Entirely up to him.

But I'd had enough of the fat turd, and needed to concentrate on the twats.

Chapter 59

I secured the folding shovel to the pack, and thought to leave the other where it lay, as promised. I'd given my word, and my word still accounted for something.

Then it was time to address the babes, while the vid cam registered every delightful detail. Like the Uni-bomber, I'd never been a fan of electronics and/or high-tech in general: Sci-fi, machinery, computers. Bunch of shit we had no business fooling with and would surely do us in one day. A blind man could see we were moving in that direction. And yet, having stated thus, there was no denying I was happy to be able to capture what was taking place in this handy manner.

"We're going to do the tango, my ex-lady loves; my former *ménage à trois* bitches. Fred Reed's version of the tango: you *running*, and me *pursuing*. Me giving you both a head start, and you hoping to stay alive by outrunning me and Payback. Or . . ." Here's where I paused. Some scribes, in certain books I read while in stir, like to call this a 'pregnant pause.' Not me. I never would. Well, I read a lot of shit while in stir, especially by a certain overrated horror schlockmeister, and others of his ilk.

"I give you a choice: Go out the way *Bondo* Grozewski just went. And see if maybe you can last long enough to dig your way to the top. What do you think? I give you both that choice."

I yanked Margie's tape from her face and she started in, cursing; the big effing mouth as always. I handed the camcorder to Monica, and did the only thing there was to do: smacked the high yellow in the face with the butt end of the rifle. And she flew; the *over-the-hill shrew* flew like she had wings. Backwards, so hard, that she landed into the large grave, the one big enough for two bitches. She was down there, stunned, silent; weeping, but not running that yap of hers. A chunk of both, upper and lower lip torn off; some of the teeth in front no longer there. Made her look like a crystal meth addict. Something like Rinelle.

I pulled out a second camcorder and got it going. Saw to it that Monica continued shooting hers as well.

"I dreamt of this . . ." Ooh, I did. Exactly this, thousands of times in my dreams; fantasies I had while lying in my bunk thinking, planning how to get back at the two man-hating, spiteful she-devils.

I gestured to Monica to help her 'life partner' up and out of the hole.

"Put the camera down for a minute. Give her a hand."

This she did. It was work, and took effort, but she managed.

Chapter 60

I had them get out of their stained and smelly clothes, then re-cuffed their wrists in front. "You're going to tiptoe through the tulips without any clothes on, and no footwear."

I tossed a pocketknife Margie's way. She caught it, then looked up. Afraid to open her trap to ask what it was for. That was fine.

"On the outside chance you have a close encounter with Bigfoot."

"Already have."

"Yeah? And I had mine with a couple of toxic vaginas." I looked at Monica. "You like *documentaries*? Exactly what we're going to do here: make a documentary. A real one. None of that fake, contrived shit, either; you know? Where you withhold footage, manipulate what's included. We're going for the *Real McCoy* here."

"This is sick." Marge could not resist the need to interject. "Your male ego can't accept the fact that two women fell in love and don't like being involved with men. You're behind the times, Fred. *Throwback.* No different from the way Frank was. This is a new world we're living in. Times have changed. There's no stigma attached to women wanting to be with women, and men with men. Accept it. You'll have to. Whether curmudgeons like you like it or not."

"I'm really going to enjoy seeing Payback tear your pee hole to pieces, bitch. In fact, that's the main reason we're putting it on video, for the playback. Multiple viewings later on."

"So you can jag off to it, no doubt."

"I'm getting a boner just thinking about this."

"Fuck you."

She spit on the ground.

"Give me a reason to put a hole through that stone heart right now, cunt, or start running for your life. I've got to take a dump. Eating that over-priced slop at Pinocchio's that they like to pass off as 'gluten-free' Italian food never did agree with me. You two ought to know about that. Should give you a head start. Between now and by the time I'm done wiping is exactly how much time you got to disappear and save your psycho ass."

Monica promised large sums of money. Whatever I wanted.

"Name it. You got it. New car, house with a pool; leads in adult features, or star in your own life story. You wanted a *ménage* with us and Lucy Ice. It's doable. She liked your style of giving oral; you know that."

"Truth is, you're an over-the-hill old ho, Monica. Both of you. Old hoes I got no use for. I got zero interest in balling a couple of bitter dykes with nasty *culos*."

"You liked Lucy. There's others like her. It can be arranged. Killing isn't always the answer."

"It sure seemed to be when Marge managed to draw me into her and her mother's scheme to do Frank Graham in, didn't it?"

"That was then. He was beating her."

"Or else she wanted it to look that way. And it worked. I was the certified chump. Scapegoat."

"It was the only way out for her. He was thoroughly abusive. You have no idea what that's like, to live under a chauvinist's thumb."

"I'm a man, therefore I wouldn't have a clue. My gender never suffers; ever."

I indicated the scar on my neck. Before she'd had a chance to say something else, I shoved a couple of pieces of paper in her face: Dog-eared newspaper articles I'd been saving since before having been released from my state subsidized cribby.

"Lower the camera and start reading."

Before Monica had so much as unraveled the one, Marge was tossing up some more lies out there.

"Let me guess: Jamal's last resort confession. How he got his career criminal ass off death row. Not much to be believed there."

Monica read in silence.

"I was standing outside your bedroom window when you asked Margie if it were true: that she and her mother had been looking for a patsy all along? And if I had been that patsy. She had denied it, just as she's denying now."

Monica looked up.

"Her mother risked losing her life if she didn't cooperate. Two wrongs don't make a right. How will taking another life solve anything?"

"Judge threw the book at me. I stood there in the courtroom listening to him list the actual offenses, then added a few imaginary ones for good measure. I was stunned. Speechless. The only thing they didn't seem to nail me for was jumping into that motel pool in my street clothes and contaminating the water with the blood from my gunshot wound. When I pointed it out to my court-appointed mouthpiece, his response was that maybe the prosecutor had overlooked it somehow and to leave it at that."

"You're out. Free to start over. Why look back? Why throw away the rest of your life? It's never too late to start over. Appreciate what you have, Fred. This takes you nowhere. Murder is wrong."

"I'm too old to give a shit about any of it."

"*Suicide* is what he's after." This was Margie's two cents worth of wisdom. Could be she was not that far off. "Once he kills us there's no going back. He'll have to take his own life, or else it's back to being caged like an animal."

"I was misled. Used. Abused. Left to die. I didn't deserve what I was put through. It seems to me you two care more for cats and dogs, four-legged creatures in general, than you do for my gender. Cunts like you are ruining society. Didn't used to be this way. You've gone too far. All you *snapper-lapping twisted sisters* have gone way overboard with this warped agenda of yours. You think I'm the only one who feels this way? I am not the only one who feels this way. Far from it. *Got an ax to grind?* So do I."

Chapter 61

Monica looked at her best friend and soulmate, waiting for answers, at least one answer that might resolve some of it. Margie, at the moment, had nothing to offer. I had Monica fold that article and hand it back.

I told her to take a gander at the other. This was the one that contained testimony from some of Margie's half-siblings: sister Tezlyn, brothers Lorenzo and Thalmus; an uncle or two.

While she read, I thought of a couple of other things. Stuff was coming at me: images mostly; words also, that echoed from deep within some chamber inside my skull. I recalled the *fracas* between Margie and Rinelle and the *faux reason* that fueled it at the Pasadena drug and booze recovery facility.

"Margie was drying out, out there in Pasadena. Rinelle showed with Jamal. There was a vicious falling out between Margie and her mother: hair-pulling and pissing; screams and creaming. Well, they were screaming at each other, while I practically found myself creaming in my boxers. That's neither here nor there, because the battle was over Margie falling for me emotionally. It wasn't supposed to happen—and her mother was freaking. I didn't get it at the time. It came to me later, much later. Added it up. It meant they'd have to start searching for another sucker to take the rap for Graham's murder. Finding the right type of sap took time and time was the one component they were in short supply."

The two exchanged glances. When Margie had nothing to offer in her defense, Monica resumed reading. She finished. Handed it back.

"Is this true about your mother, Margie?"

"I don't know. And besides, what difference does it make at this point? Fred got dumped and will find a way to justify killing us for it, out of spite; spite and vengeance. You heard him: it's about payback. Nothing else. What Rinelle did or didn't do has nothing to do with Fred's agenda!"

"Rinelle was the personification of the term Black Widow. Poisoned who knows how many of her hubbies and/or unfortunate gentlemen callers. Graham was just another worthless 'male loser' who needed to be put out of his misery for the cause. Cash was in short supply. It's always in short supply, no matter how much of it dope fiends get their hands on. Rinelle and Jamal's craving for crack and meth was out of control. You read the articles: Jamal was a pusher who didn't know how to keep from getting high on his supply. Owed plenty to those he got his shit from. Graham's life insurance, plus bank account and property he owned was clearly the bull's eye on the bounty hunter's back."

Monica said her 'life partner's' name, desperately waiting for another denial. It came, but it was as lame as those before it.

"Lies, Monica. Jamal created this false confession because the DA's office promised him a deal. It saved him; the so-called confession spared his miserable life. Got him off death row, like I said and been saying: *He saved his own ass with a pack of fabrications.*"

I saw an opportunity to jump in.

"What reason did your siblings have to *'fabricate'* anything, Marge?"

"Pay off."

"By whom, Marge? How?"

"Jamal's book contract with a major New York publisher. He won't get a dime, but they sure stand to."

"Were Jamal's nosebleeds fabricated? Or were they caused by boric acid he caught Rinelle dumping into his *Wheaties*?"

"Lies to save his ass. Shave time off his sentence."

"Hardly."

"Got him off death row."

"Bodies were unearthed, re-examined. Antifreeze was discovered in Mario and others. Your stepfather never died of a heart-attack, did he?"

Margie said nothing.

"Prison shrinks had an expression they were partial to: *Cognitive dissonance*. Ever heard of it, Margie? Any idea what it means?"

"No. Why don't you enlighten us? Since you're the one who entered the big house a dumb-ass and came out a wise-ass."

"You know the truth, yet insist on deceiving yourself."

"Deceive this."

Margie stood there defiantly. Middle finger raised. She was good at it. Feisty Margie of old was back. Her true nature tough to shake, after all. Not unlike a rattlesnake taking on a new skin after it had slithered out of the old. The poison remained. It was still a venomous reptile. What had been my immediate reaction to Rinelle years before, pretty much. And twisted Margie had been contaminated by her. So had plenty of others out there, no doubt. Society. Scrambled and fried. Welcome to the carnival of warped minds and disfigured anatomies. You had a choice: tolerate and learn to exist in it, or opt out entirely. I must've been leaning toward the latter, like Marge said.

"What it was always about: you and Rinelle giving a worthless fuck like me the finger. Getting her off the hook with Jamal and his source. I happened to come along. Ready-made heartsick sucker. Scapegoat. It was perfect."

". . . No."

"Took you a while."

"You were and you weren't."

"Which?'

"Initially. Then I fell in love."

"For a while."

"You saw the battles I had with Rinelle. We bloodied one another silly."

"Granted; it was awesome burlesque. Some of the best. Motive appeared muddled, but it was entertaining to watch."

"The reason for my attempted suicide. I was conflicted. Didn't want you involved. Rinelle kept pushing, insisting. She had no choice, really. She owed. What the battles were about. She was under pressure to pay up. I sent what I could; what I was able to get Graham to give up. It wasn't enough; it was never enough—no matter how much was sent."

"Indecisiveness that lasted about, what?—five seconds?"

"Weeks; months. You know this."

"Bullshit."

"They threatened to start amputating her fingers—one by one—unless I got with it and delivered. Frank had to go. Jamal and his low-born thugs sent that finger and threatened to do more unless I did as they asked. I did what I could to keep it from you, hoping you wouldn't see it."

Who sent the finger was questionable at best. I let that part of it go just then.

"No, you left it where I was sure to find it."

"To what purpose?"

"To make it easier to justify to yourself the double-cross you planned to pull off later on: You stabbing me in the back. Exactly what this is about. It didn't work. Actually, it's laughable."

"You would find humor in it."

"Finger was a phony. Either you or Rinelle must've greased some underhanded undertaker's palm along the way to provide said male finger, then painted it with nail polish to make it look plausible."

"How was I to know where it came from?—who sent it?"

"Oh, you knew. This was worked out between you and your mother. I'd stake my life on it. I'll go so far as to claim that you were glad she was offed finally. Made it possible for you to lay your hands on the entire pot of gold—at the end of the blood-stained rainbow. *Bingo.* Your way of finally getting back at her for shoving your underage ass at degenerates old enough to be your grandfather."

"Finger may not have been hers, doesn't mean that the threat on her life wasn't real. You saw Jamal, what he looked like. We both know how it ended for Rinelle and what he did to her."

"When he caught her trying to feed him roach killer. Still doesn't explain the lies at the end, ratting me out when it was *you* who *stuck* the needle in Graham. It was you insisted on rat poison, not me. It was *you* who put *antifreeze* in his thermos long before I happened on the scene. Like I said before: I was a Johnny-come-lately in all of it. Certified chump."

"I told the insurance company what they needed to hear—for the payout. Only by then it was too late to save her."

"In that case, how come I never saw my slice of the pie? Not that it excuses the betrayal."

"What good was it going to do you in prison? I had a life to live. You were in a cage. Well provided for by the state."

"*Goddamn, you're ignorant.* It was life and death every minute of every hour of every day of every week of every excruciating, mother-fucking month of every year I was inside."

"You're not satisfied with my answers, the truth as I know it, then all I can offer up is this. Choke on it, fucker."

She had balls. Because the finger was back. Where the backbone came from, I had no idea or was even able to come close to explaining. Was I amused by the gesture? Some. Payback wasn't, and went at her, digging his fangs into her right ankle. Margie smacked at the dog, hard. Not with the knife, but her free hand. Had she used the knife at this juncture she would have been dead on the spot. End of story. But she hadn't and her reward was she got to go on breathing. *For the time being.*

"Don't like dogs, bitch? He's way better than a pile of shit like you."

I stowed the camera. Slung the rifle over my shoulder and had the shotgun up, aiming. At this close range I preferred going the shotgun route. Marge did not hesitate this time, and limped off.

The dog barked, vicious mother that he was. Wanted Margie's hide. I rubbed the back of his neck to calm him down. He did. To a degree. Then noticed Monica, and would have settled for her easily enough. I held on to Payback's leash. Monica jumped back, her face streaked with tears and blood.

I undid my belt buckle, and squatted.

Chapter 62

I reminded Monica to get the video camera going. Did suggest to keep it wide and that I didn't want jarring once we began our trek after her lesbian pal. She was sobbing, shaking uncontrollably.

"Get a grip, or I'll bury you right now."

I wasn't raising my voice. There was no need for it. She knew I meant business. My rage, my hatred/loathing was one hundred percent pure. The only problem in this area of loathing came down to trying to decide which one of these *'femme fatales'* I loathed more.

"See, that was the one thing that was tough for me: concluding which one of you I resented and wanted to deep-six ever deeper: *Her* or *you*? *You* or *her*? It went back and forth like that all those years while in the joint. Everything else was worked out. I even had backup/contingency plans, but had never been able to decide which one of you ball-busters I wanted to see scream out the loudest; which one deserved the greater intensity of suffering. I'm still at a loss, years later. Standing right here, looking at your worthless fucking face, can't decide."

Then it occurred to me: the long strands, filthy and dangling over her eyes might interfere with her ability to get good footage.

I drew the dagger from the scabbard. That got her to stop sobbing at least.

"Lower the camera."

I held the blade up, near her face, then holding clumps of hair in the other hand, cut quite a bit of it all around. Chopped it off. She looked like shit. Well, she looked like shit lately anyway, but this made her appear atrocious. So be it.

"I want some *decent footage* of this."

She nodded her head.

I double-checked the items: shotgun, rifle, rope, handguns, ammo, rubber mallet, duct tape, water, biscuits for Payback, power bars for myself. I'd been able to stuff quite a bit of it into the backpack. Payback continued to growl at Monica and it was clear enough to me he wanted a piece of her, possibly more than a piece. Seemed like he wanted to tear her apart.

She was naked, no shoes. I looked at my watch. How much time had I given Margie? Twenty, twenty-five minutes?

"Should we give her another five, Monica dear? What do you think?"

She wasn't saying.

"Don't you think she deserves five more minutes?"

"What difference would it really make?"

I nodded. Had to agree.

"You'll kill her the way you killed Mr. Grozewski."

"No, I'm afraid it's going to be a lot more painful . . . for the both of you. It's going to be excruciatingly painful. Because, you see, I was emotionally involved . . . and felt some sympathy should have been forthcoming; felt I was owed something, a little more than what I got, at least. What I got, in fact, was zero. Nothing. That's what you're going to get here from me. *Exactly. Nothing.*"

She didn't say anything.

"Well, then, we got us an old whore to find. The hunt is on."

Chapter 63

I let Payback take a good whiff of Margie's panties, and off we went.
He tugged and yanked and growled, pulling on the leather leash. It was all
I could do to hold him back, keep him from causing me to trip on my own
feet. There were rocks out here, crevices, cacti, twigs, branches and a few
dead Joshua trees that had been uprooted by a vicious storm or two over
the years, or else old age had been the real culprit. Possibly both.

I reminded Monica that I didn't need to be in the shot. Mainly I
wanted footage of her lesbian friend, once we got close enough.

"Depending on what Payback does. Try to stay in front of me, better
yet—off to the side. I don't need to be in any of the shots."

"When do I start?"

"I'll let you know."

She was to my right, walking alongside this way. She was holding the
camera in her hand, waiting for word from me. I happened to look down
at her mud-caked feet. There were cuts.

Now, I had no idea what Margie might attempt to retaliate with. Yes,
she was a woman, but she was no meek little chickie, either, not at 5ft 11,
and those strong thighs and buttocks. She didn't have powerful shoulders,
this was true, but I also knew she could throw a punch. Saw it with my
own peepers, many moons ago, when we were young and pretty and she
and her mother were engaged in fisticuffs. Then I remembered the time I
stopped her from poisoning Graham's kids. Fact was both of these twats

were twisted. Then you had me: with a crack right down the center of my psyche too blatant to ignore. I used to be in denial about it. No more. No point. What for? We were *'triple threats'* all right. These hoes were at the end of their rope, and if they wanted to stay alive you knew they had to try to pull something, anything. It behooved me to stay alert. Like in the fuckin' jungle, or as you drove a transport through some village. You never knew when that sniper's bullet would pierce your helmet and park itself in your scared shitless brain.

Anything was possible.

It was then I thought to look up, at the trees, all around. That's what you did: kept looking around, all the time. Left, right, in front of you— and up into the trees. Came down to you or Charley.

Was she dumb enough to actually climb up a tree? She'd be dead meat for sure if she did that. There was no way Payback would miss it.

My good buddy continued to tug, but then he'd go off to the left, double-back, go to the right; then returned to where I stood and headed on in a straight line—as if he was walking point. Well, could be he was. Point dog. Wanted her ass. Wanted blood. Payback could tell they were no good. That simple. I'd got taken in years before: by the curves, tits, pussy and *culo*. And with Monica? It was even more than that; she'd been far more conniving: when she laid all that fake sweetness on me. And I'd thought: *Lifesaver. Hope.* The light at the end of the tunnel. A way out; a way to rescue myself and have something like a clean and normal life. She was sane, and I'd needed someone normal and sane. She appeared to be, anyway. Good-hearted. Fair-minded. Fuck. What a chump. That *facade* had me conned; suckered me in, and I'd let my guard down. Never up to that point. Had always managed to stay alert when dealing with humans. I knew it was a world of smiling two-faced snakes. The *T&T* reeled me in. *Tits and Tang. BJs.* It was more than that. A state of serenity. Peace of mind. Sure.

I looked at her just then. Easily hated her more than ever. Despicable? She was that—and some. I despised the off-kilter *effing lesbo* more than I could ever state here. It wasn't so much that she had turned gay and taken up with that other duplicitous witch; as stated before: I didn't give a rat's ass who was gay or what people did between the sheets. None of that shit meant a thing to me. Women liked to eat pussy? Their business. Men enamored with the penis? Their call, not mine. Was zippo to me. Waste of time to even think about. Saw it in stir: males doing the nasty with each other. Who gave a good goddamn, man? The whole effing sex thing was not only overrated, but utterly moronic. I said it: *Moronic.* With a capital *M.* Very often— *or at the least*: more often than not—we were mentally defective creatures and carried on as such. So, no, the fact they devolved into lesbians, or say, always had been, though it was latent, it was the fact they'd *turned on me*—and not only TURNED, but treated me as though I were less-than-human, simply for having been born with a pair of balls and a prick. This was exactly where my disdain came from, this rage that had been brewing and escalating over the years. To say I had loathing wouldn't come close to stating how much hatred I harbored toward the two ball-busting sacks of female waste.

And as far as women went in general? This world wouldn't be much without them. Hell, it wasn't much anyway. But am saying, life would be just about a total waste of fucking time without the female to spice things up and make existence interesting.

So there you have it: for all those man-hating bull dykes out there. You know the type am talking about. The pig ugly, perpetually angry wenches with the hairy upper lip, who can't seem to get through a day without blaming all that ails this universe on the male. Those worthless, hateful *bags of hog snot* I can do without. Those are the bitches this world would have been way better off without; those are the *hate-filled shrews* who cause so much grief among the average male and female who merely wish to get along and know how to appreciate one another.

But types like Margie and Monica? I got no use for. In fact, nothing would make me happier than to slice them up; make them suffer like no one has ever suffered. Their type like to talk about: *Hell hath no fury like a woman scorned* . . . Really? Get ready, because I'm going to show you what real fury is about. Fasten your seat belts, motherfuckers, because the *Freddie Reed Wrath Express* is headed your way.

Chapter 64

Payback got my attention again with all the tugging and jumping and growling. He wanted to sink his fangs into flesh.

I didn't know what sense it made, but I suppose he knew what he was doing. Could've been the way Marge had been scampering along: undecided. *Zig-zagging.* Then thought her chances were best if she kept on in a straight path. So this is the way we trudged on, straight ahead, but after I'd taken a look at the cell screen to see what, if anything, the hidden video cam aimed at Grozewski's grave picked up. No movement, that I could tell. Didn't know if he was alive, or dead—or if he had a real shot at clawing his way to the top. It was up to him. All of it. Entirely up to him.

I followed Payback's lead. It was a nice crisp morning. After all that rain. Clear blue sky. *Azure.* Unusual for usually hazy Southern California.

Chapter 65

Monica stubbed her left foot and winced and had to stop. I let her. In fact, I did better than that: I had her sit on a boulder, lifted the foot to take a better look. Poured water on it to wash the mud and blood off; then I took out a Band-Aid and applied it to the cut. She looked at me without saying anything. The expression on her dirty face said plenty: *Why do this if you intend to kill me later?*

"I especially need you to run the camera for this portion of it. Would really like you to stay healthy long enough to nail the temperamental twat. Of course, I'd like you to stay fairly fit for when we start your phase of the adventure."

Didn't mention that I had other things in mind for the duo—to test this bond that they had between them; this love and loyalty and dedication. What would take place between them when it came time to decide, choose between life or death? Would they turn on each other? Go for blood? It would be interesting to see. I'd be running the cam for that part of it.

She fought back sobs.

"Psycho bitch from hell. Two of them. Never shed a tear when I was hurting and being sent up the river; but your dyke friend gets a scratch, or you stub your toe and it's cause to go on a crying jag."

The dog wanted a chance at her. I held him back.

"See, even he knows you're dung." I turned away, spit, then looked at her. "Cry me a fucking ocean, bitch. Move your ass. Let's go."

We moved out.

Chapter 66

Payback tugged another time, hard, nearly causing me to trip on a log that had been lying diagonally across our path. I cursed, staring at him. He seemed to be saying he hadn't meant it, but merely wanted to sink his teeth into the ho we were chasing after.

I kissed him on the snout. "Forget it, pal. I understand."

I happened to look at Monica. Tears were flowing again, snot. She wiped with the back of her forearm.

"I risked going to jail over that dog of yours that time. Chambray? Remember that psycho dog. I never knew why Chambray was so angry and fucked up. I mean, I understood, I related because that was me; my whole fucking life—but I didn't get what had caused her to become like that. I don't know why I felt that way about it, because there was no mystery to it: she had you for a mistress. You, and whoever else had been abusive to her."

"I'd had to leave her back in Phoenix with some people for a few months. Something must have happened to her. I never mistreated her. I saved her from a trailer trash family as a pup."

"Or else your own family fucked her up, the same way they fucked you up. Wished I could have spotted your hatred toward the male early on. I would have bailed. Right away. Would not have stuck around. Nope. I suspected you had plenty of bitterness in you . . . only I kept hoping my gut instinct was wrong."

I spit on the ground, took a sip of water. Poured some down Payback's throat. Gave him a dog biscuit.

"I loved Chambray. . . ."

"Love, Monica? What's that? You loved me, too, as I recall."

She said nothing. Tears rolled.

"Margie means that much to you?"

It took her a while to answer.

"You know she does. That pocketknife isn't going to do her much good out here, with all these wild animals roaming, snakes."

"We'll see how much she means to you. . . ."

The dog jerked on the leash; impatient to get going. I held him back, just a second. I needed to take another look at my cell screen and the image being picked up by the vid cam back at Grozewski's grave. It was a decent enough angle, shooting down from high up in a nearby tree. Although the camera was primarily pointed at the grave the former dick was in, I'd left it wide enough to cover plenty of the area. And just to be on the safe side, I had a backup cam aiming at the general area from a different angle.

There was movement. And then some. Looked like fatso had managed to burrow his way to the surface finally. I watched him yank the hose out of his jaw and toss it. Had to give the man credit. Cuffed wrists, many pounds of heavy dirt on top of him; dirt in his ears, nose and eyes, and he managed to make it to the surface.

I stood there appreciating the effort. He lay on top of the grave, on his back, gasping for air, sobbing; covered in grime and whatnot, gasping and sobbing.

After a while, he stopped the blubbering, looked around, making sure I wasn't anywhere near, and crawled toward the jug of water. Uncapped it and gulped down plenty, recapped it and reached for the shovel. He staggered to his feet, and limped out of sight.

Okay. Fine. Earned it, didn't he? I wasn't sweating. Let's see how far he gets. About the only thing that concerned me was Monica's kid, and maybe Bruno's boyfriend. Not Bix, but Percival Balsley. I also wondered what Aldo, the Pizzeria manager, might think up. I had no idea.

I played the footy back for Monica, to let her see. She looked up afterwards.

"Will you let him be now? Will you let him live?"

I said nothing.

"After all he's been put through, after all the pain you caused him . . . doesn't he deserve a break?"

"Sure. He deserves a break; the same break you three gave me."

"So you're showing it to me just to torment me."

"Showing it to point out how *determined* and *resilient* humans can be at times. This was exactly the kind of determination that kept me going all those years in stir: wanting my taste of vengeance."

"Was it worth it?"

"You have no idea how sweet."

"Margie was right. Only this is beyond sick."

"Because you're the ones being subjected to it. When it was being done to me it was par for the course; nothing unusual. I didn't rate. When you were rending my heart to pieces . . . it was no big deal. . . . It was, in fact, entertainment. You were amused by it. I saw the doc you made afterwards; saw the footage. I was the laughing stock in the joint because of the lies you and that cunt spread about me. This scar . . ." I yanked on my collar, as I had before in their studio. This time I held it a while. "Shiv attack, as a result of your documentary. Punk decided to test my mettle. So don't talk to me about breaks, asshole, and how sick someone is. Turds like you, and her, is the real reason this world is so fucked up. On the surface: nice and calm, so decent. But below—once you look below the thin veneer— is where the bile lies."

I flipped the lid to close the video screen, and we headed in Margie's direction. Payback was happy about that.

Chapter 67

The cell phone in the right pocket of my cargo pants went off. I dug it out. Modigliani. Texting. Again.

Mom, why won't you answer? I am worried. Where are you? Please respond. Let me know that you're all right. Love you, Mom. Modi.

I showed it to Monica. She choked back sobs.

"Let's stop this. Fred. Now. While you have a chance. Bruno is alive. You won't be tried for murder, at least."

"I won't be tried for anything. That's the plan. I paid. More than my share of dues. *I paid.*"

"Enough is enough."

The second I stowed her cell, the one in the other pocket went off. It was Aldo, of all people. *Aldo.* What did any of this have to do with him? Pizzeria manager. Yes, the name of that greasy spoon was *Pinocchio's*, but this did not excuse him sticking his nose in it.

Margie, we need to know that you're all right. Margie? Please let us know. Something. Anything. People are worried.

I thought it made better sense to respond than not to:

We're on our way to see a doctor friend of Bruno's. We both have a terrible case of the running shits. Thanks to you. Hoping the doctor will be able to give us something for it.

Then the text signal sounded again. This time it was her son.

What's this doctor's name, Mom?

My comeback? *Dr. Feelgood.*

Where are you, Mom?

I wasn't going to respond after the above, but then thought: What the hell. The kid is worried.

Beverly Hills. We're fine. And quit worrying so much. Love, Mom.

I closed it, placed it on a boulder, reached for the mallet—and smashed the cell to bits. Cops had a way of tracing these things, even when not in use. In case Modi had attempted to file a missing persons report. I dug the other cell out, and did the same to it: crushed the crap out of it, then swept the pieces into the wind, hard, with the back of my forearm. Watched them scatter.

The texting had become annoying. Made me wonder if the kid had gone to the rollers. I was being pushed into actually turning into a serial killer—and this was the last thing I wanted. My conclusion: if they showed; if the busybodies appeared: Monica's son Modi, Aldo—and, possibly, Percival. If those two were up in arms over this, so then was Percy. Had to be. I'd have to deal with them—and whoever else they had with them. *Five-0?* I didn't know. This would make me a serial killer. For sure. That many bodies? That many lives snuffed? Yes. *If it went that far.* I had no idea that it would—or wouldn't.

"You can't kill all of us, Fred. They did nothing to you. My son, and Mr. Picasso."

"Let's hope they don't get out here and find us, before I've had a chance to take care of you two shrewish wenches. On the other hand, should they appear . . . who knows what might happen."

"You're seriously ill. You know that, don't you?"

"Let's see: I'm ill, and you're not? You and that other twisted old crow are perfectly normal. What was done to me—the *'scrotum sack'* in this ménage—is acceptable to you. That how you see it?"

"You broke my heart. I loved you. You took that love and tampered with it, testing my trust, until it finally turned to contempt. No different from what my mother was put through by one heartless cad after another."

"And your ex-hubby, no doubt."

"Yes."

"That's how it is. At last. The picture comes into focus. That's how you justified what I was subjected to?"

"The last one conned her out of her house, cleaned out her bank account; broke her heart and took everything she had. Disappeared. Never to be heard from again. She had a nervous breakdown. Was in therapy for years. She died a broken old woman."

"That might explain why you turned out the way you did. Doesn't excuse it, but it'll do. Or else you had *lesbo* tendencies all along. *Latent*. Bitter. Spiteful. Toward my gender. Waited for the slightest reason to excuse unleashing it. Doubt you ever had genuine love for that kid of yours. Modi? Should've been born female. Females are superior to the male in every way. Your take on things. What's the other psychopathic female's reason for being the way she is?"

"Her stepfather was a skirt-chasing whore monger. He drank."

"All the blame falls on daddy. Her mentally imbalanced, drug addicted *Black Widow Mommy* had nothing to do with it. That how that old song goes? Blame all of it on the male of the species, that it? No matter how many dudes took a dirt nap as a result of her one of a kind, Rinelle Rossi concoction."

"You had a lot coming to you."

"Not half as much as you two spiteful *culos* were so eager to mete out."

Chapter 68

There was a boulder about two hundred feet up ahead of us. Gut instinct indicated it was time to have the camera back in action. I gave the nod, and turned Payback loose. What sounded like Margie giving up a shriek on the other side soon after was followed by a yelp that made chills crawl up my spine.

We hurried over to discover Payback lying on his side with the knife hilt sticking out of his left temple. Next to zero life left in the mutt. Marge stood over him, pure rage in her eyes. Arms and legs streaked with blood.

There was no choice but to shoot him. Add this hurt on top of all the others.

I had her retract the pocketknife. I detached the folding shovel from my pack and tossed it at her feet and had the over-the-hill ballbuster dig a hole to bury my friend in. I relieved Monica of the camcorder and had her help out. Payback was lowered into the ground and covered up. I retrieved the shovel.

"There's only one way out of this for either of you. . . ." I tossed the same type of pocketknife to Monica. "Go to it. Carve each other up, or . . . take your chances with this." I indicated the shotgun. It was also time for the camcorder to be back on. Footy would be needed of the ensuing segment. I waited. I grinned, and I waited.

"Got a choice. . . . Up to you."

Chapter 69

There was some superficial slashing and non-life-threatening stabbing and kicks and hair-pulling and spitting, even peeing. Lots of screaming and tears. But Margie, having been assaulted and bloodied by Payback earlier, turned out to be no match for Monica.

She was down, on her back, out of her mind, but not so crazy that she still did not wish to live at this point. Monica was kneeling beside her, frothing mouth and face over hers, knife held against Margie's throat. It was tense, good and tense. I had a boner. Nothing like witnessing two naked psycho bitches going at each other. No denying my need for it: *blood lust.* Only I wondered what the bitch was waiting for.

"Finish her."

She wouldn't. She couldn't. Tears flowed. She was sighing. Gasping.

Tossed her knife aside, clutching her belly. Then rolled over on her back for a while, trying to catch her breath. Then a moment later she was embracing the stunned and wordless (for a change) Margie, sobbing in her bosom and kissing her face: tears and dirt.

"I am so sorry, dearest Margie. Can you ever forgive me?"

It was touching; and it was also comical. Because Margie was a *woman* she was *worth* crying over; she was *worth* empathy, *worth* being embraced and supported. I, on the other hand, hadn't been worth a damn when I'd been down, hurting, struggling to hold on by a mere thread.

Fuck 'em. Men can be wrathful. My actions here proved it. Many times over. Freddy's wrath. *A Dead Man's Wrath.* Would have made a nice title for this tale. Even better than *Night Sweats.* But enough was enough. I'd had my fill of the dykes and their all-too-sentimental affection for each other. I pitched the heavy rope at her, had her tie it about Margie's upper torso and then I had the shaken survivor drag her loving pal back to the grave, where both were dumped, not unlike refuse that they were, and covered up—without benefit of a hose to breathe through. I made myself scarce.

Chapter 70

I monitored quite a bit of what followed on my cell. Grozewski leapt out from behind bushes with his shovel and water jug, and started digging in the general area Monica had been buried.

After a while, feeling frustrated by the cell's less than adequate image of what unfolded, I did reposition myself, although remaining concealed, close enough to the action to be able to capture more of it with the camcorder in my immediate possession. Here's where I got bold to the point of temporarily abandoning the oft-sought wide angle and zoomed in. I wanted detail. I'd read, or heard, somewhere along the way that 'detail was god.' So be it. I fooled with the zoom. Moved in for a bit, and kept it there; then I zoomed out some. I was no filmmaker. Certainly had no desire for it. Now or ever. But I was also fairly certain experimenting with the zoom in this manner would meet my needs.

Growzewski had tossed the shovel aside and had started in with his bare hands, clawing and scraping at the dirt with his trembling fingers, sobbing the entire time. I watched snot, sweat and tears drip from his chin and cheeks.

He got to her face. Helped pull her out. Handed her the jug of water for a quick gulp while he dug away to rescue their pal.

Monica was one anxious wreck, looking around constantly. The fact that Bondo was ignoring her unsettled state enervated her further. This only resulted in underscoring his own shaky demeanor and he reminded her to calm down, that they needed to help Margie get out.

"He'll kill us."

"He's gone."

"He is just waiting for us to help Marge so that he can murder all three of us. That's what this is about. Whole purpose. He's *psycho. Sadistic.*"

"No. He won't. He's gone."

"*How do you know?*"

"Why do you think he left the shovel behind?" Grozewski pointed to the jug. "*And that!* Would he want us to have water to drink if he intended to kill us?" Then producing a pair of car keys on a keyring, he dangled them in front of her stunned face. "That's right: keys to his van. Left on the seat. *Would he want us to have the van if he didn't want us to live?*"

She looked at him, while he resumed shoveling dirt.

"That's right. It came from Fred."

"How do you know those are keys to the van?"

"How do you know they're not? Even if they're not, it would be easy enough to hot wire."

"Makes no sense. What's he going to do out here in the middle of nowhere without transportation?"

Bondo shrugged. "He's suicidal. Let's hope he kills himself. Who cares what he does?" He urged her to help him dig. "Please. *Monica.*"

She snapped out of it, and assisted. Frantically.

"Thank you."

"The nightmare is finally over. We get my sweetie out, give her some water to drink, and get her some help; get all three of us some help. And turn him in. Throw him back in prison, where an animal like that belongs."

"You talk too much."

"*I talk too much?*"

The former dick looked around. "You're saying way too much."

She bent down, started brushing/shoveling dirt aside with her hands. Then just as suddenly, yanked the shovel out of his and pushed him away.

She had to be the one to rescue her best friend and lover, not some male, even though he was gay and really had been a good pal of theirs for years.

Margie's face appeared. Frantic, panic-stricken, in desperate need of oxygen. Monica wiped dirt and pebbles from her face and neck. Leaned in to give her mouth-to-mouth. Helped her sit up, then gradually, allowing Bondo to lend a hand this time, pulled her up and out. Offered the jug of water. With their additional assistance, Margie managed to stand on her feet. Coughed, non-stop. Disoriented. Had no idea where she was, or who the two people beside her were. Monica embraced her. Bondo attempted to. Margie wanted nothing to do with either one. Cursed in a mixture of Spanglish at them, as well as the dirt in her eyes that she had a difficult time getting rid of.

I was at the rear of the van at this point, where I stayed put, eyeing the proceedings. I'd had no idea, none, that I would let them walk . . . until it happened; up until this very moment. I always claimed I was no serial killer. Was this proof enough? What I wanted, above all else, was payback. And this I got. And then some.

Chapter 71

I watched the scene transpire. Not sure why exactly, because I'd had enough of it. There wasn't going to be any killing. I didn't want to go down that path, after all. It was time to call it quits. And when I saw how manic Margie had become, I knew it was the right decision. She attacked him, then Monica. Margie had gone insane. Monica nearly there, same as Bondo. Batshit crazy. She grabbed at Monica's hair and yanked and wouldn't stop, until Grozewski stepped in to break it up. Shoved them apart. But then Margie screamed, cursing, and scratched at his face, pummeling him with her fists. Then it was Monica's turn to come between the two of them. It went on. They ran away from her, down the path, toward where the van was parked, and Margie went after them, picking up rocks to pitch at them. She picked up a sizable switch, slashed at the air with it, and tore after her friends.

Chapter 72

I stepped out from behind the front of the van, aimed the shotgun at Bondo, and let go with a blast. Blood and bone and waste spattered Monica's upper body and face. She screamed. I aimed at her torso, squeezed the trigger, and she disintegrated into way too many grisly pieces herself.

Margie walked over, cursing at her 'stepfather': *Me*. Now *I* was her *Daddy*. I aimed at her skull to shut that motor mouth up, and let go. The first volley took her head right off. I followed it up with another aimed at her torso before her body hit the ground.

I retrieved the camcorder from where I'd had it perched atop a nearby stump. Scraped their pieces up with a shovel and dumped the viscera and limbs into that old bucket I had and then dropped the mess in a hole I'd dug not far from there. It took so many trips that I lost count after the first dozen or so, but I got it done.

Initially I had considered planting them in the same grave Payback (presently re-christened *'Debt-Free'*) was in simply because it appeared to be closer, or was it? Blame it on exhaustion. No way was my friend's final resting place closer. Not only that. Why insult the dog? He deserved better.

The physical labor part of the task over, there appeared a need for this avenger to take a dump, but before doing so another need, more urgent than that one came into play: I had to urinate. And so I did. Whipped it out and pissed over their remains. Yes. I made sure to spread it around, giving all three their equal share.

I filled the hole back up. Well, you had to treat the dead with some respect. Why not? Then, of course, number #2 was on: a need to take that dump. Yes, I'd crapped earlier, but you know how it goes: some days you had to shit twice. Life.

I undid my trousers, squatted over the area where Monica was down there, squeezed out a good one, then I moved on over to where chunks and limbs of her female friend lay in the ground below me, and liberated another sizable log. *Coup de grace*, I believe it's called. The ultimate kiss-off. You might also say there had been a need to 'autograph' their final resting place. This was Hollywood, after all, the 'Dream Factory'—and the Dream Factory always was full of shit anyway.

Chapter 73

I drove the van toward the edge of a cliff, shoved it in 'P' and got out.
Opened the rear door, poured lighter fluid over the mattress and set the
mattress on fire, and closed the door. I walked to the driver's side, climbed
back in, shoved the shifter into 'D', and watched the van roll toward the
edge. Flames billowed in back of me. I couldn't think of a more perfect
way to go out. I'd always had this fear of heights, fear of flying, fear of
being burned alive—and this was my way of overcoming and facing all
three of my fears head-on.

I stayed calm, collected. Truly. At peace. The van inched closer and
closer to the edge. It rolled, gradually, but it made progress, as did the
fire, crackling. I could hear the wheels going over and crushing what
sounded like glass shards and dry clumps of mud and gravel. Just as we
reached the very edge, and the front end was over the cliff and began
tipping downward and the front wheels cleared the edge itself, I shoved
my door open and leapt out and watched the rest of it go over, and nose-
dive to the abyss below, where it was engulfed by flame. Front end
crushed like an accordion, and the rest billowing: fire and black smoke.
I may have waited for the explosion that never happened. Hollywood
movies were so much bullshit and outright lies. Cars rarely exploded.
Sure, now and then. It was fairly uncommon. But the mother did burn.
I have to tell ya. All out. Fire.

Why hadn't I stayed in the van? Simple: Depredation. Scavengers.
Vultures, lizards, scorpions, coyotes and other scavengers would have

appeared eventually to pick at my bones. I couldn't allow that sort of thing, not after what I'd been through. Nope. Still had a bit of self-respect left. Some. Not much. Some.

Chapter 74

The deed is done. The Piper was paid. Some will tell you revenge is a dish best served cold. I can't comment one way or another. The Germans have a word for it: *schadenfreude*. The Italian version is *contrapasso*. All I know is it felt good. Gave me a certain satisfaction to bury these sacks of manure. That's what they were to me. Not even human. Could be I'm not much myself. Could be none of us is. I would let all those idiot philosophers that I read over the years while in stir contemplate that pile of worthless turds.

Me? After retrieving the tree-cams, as well as anything else connected to what took place out here, I made my way to the pre-dug grave that awaited—far from there. I hadn't wanted to be anywhere near them and I thought this was fine. All I had to do now was decide the way I wanted to check out. Options were available. Too many to go into. Alas, it came down to cyanide, or shotgun blast (à la Ernie Hemingway). Now, my sole purpose of contemplating the shotgun route is to circumvent any pointless suffering. I figure I've had more than my share of it already. Should this make it difficult to ID the body later on, match DNA? Depends how long it takes them to locate my bones. That basic & that simple. Buy it or don't buy it.

I have a plywood board rigged to the left of the grave that the dirt is banked against so that all I have to do is lie down in the hole, kick the two-by-four that supports the plywood out of the way a moment before the blast, and the dirt will pour in over me and fill the hole up. My purpose for this phase of it? As before, at the edge of the cliff and why I leapt out of the van before it went over: to prevent depredation. That is a postmortem diss I have no use for. On the other hand, should it happen anyway, so be it. Nothing to be done there.

Chapter 75

In the end, I'm just another peckerwood with my pecker in one hand and a shotgun in the other. I will stroke my groin for one final blast of Twinkie filling, while replaying the footage in all its grisly and gruesome detail on the camcorder screen, then—hopefully, in tandem—squeeze the trigger for the best orgasm of all.

You see, the narrative was always moving in this direction. What more could any man hope for? Well, he might hope for something else, something in addition, even better—but he wouldn't get it.

If you're holding the stack of paper that contains the full disclosure regarding the ménage and how it imploded, then someone has found my remains, or at least discovered the manuscript. On the other hand, if you have yet to come across the confession, and that's what this screed is, after all, a confession, then the fools are still searching.

THE END

LUSTMORD:

Anatomy of a Serial Butcher
Book One (of Two)

By KIRK ALEX

Blurb & Novel Excerpt

*Who knew the minister next door
was also a sadistic predator?*

Cecil Omar Biggs is not your average man of the cloth. By day, he appears to be a hardworking preacher, but once night descends upon the quiet Southern California neighborhood where Biggs resides, his darker self emerges. Living a double life as a sex fiend and brutal murderer, he enjoys luring innocent victims into his basement lair by any means possible.

Converting an old house into a church, Biggs becomes the perfect wolf in sheep's clothing, which also puts him in the ideal position to attract his unsuspecting prey. He lives to satisfy his sinister appetites without remorse or limits, indulging in his more violent tendencies as soon as the sun goes down by torturing and killing the women he abducts in his dungeon of doom.

But how long can Biggs keep up the nice-guy-next-door pretense while secretly living as a homicidal maniac? And what happens when the locals start suspecting that there's more to this seemingly harmless Bible-thumper than meets the eye?

Chapter 1

They were into it. Heard more than he wanted to.

"J.J., don't!"

"Shut your mouth, whore!"

"I'll be good! I promise, J.J.!"

"I told you to shut your hole!"

"Don't hit me, J.J. You better not hit me no more!"

"I'll beat you to death! Filthy heifer cunt!" Slaps and screams followed. "Why, you ain't even a good whore! Where's my whiskey money, bitch? Spent on shoes and ice cream for that worthless little shit? Why come? Since when are the little bastard's wants more important than mine?"

More slaps followed, screaming. The next sound was the male's, a deep grunt, as though on the receiving end himself. Furniture was thrown, dishes. The woman shrieked.

"We're out of ass-wipe, over-the-hill heifer, and you got nerve to waste money on ice cream and shoes for the little pissy!" Dogs barked; a real ruckus was in progress up there. The boy pretty much ignored it all. Went about in a calm way burning his spiders, tearing wings off flies.

The view from where he stood at the grimy rear window on this tenement landing between the third and fourth floors gave one about as much hope and peace of mind as the hell going on up on the fourth floor: a back parking lot with cracks in the pavement, pot holes and loose cement chunks and gravel that had, over time, become the unofficial dumping site for neighborhood wrecks. Autos of all makes and sizes, pickup trucks, vans, gutted. Some without doors and windshields or wheels, had been abandoned to rust on wood or cinder blocks, bricks, piled rocks.

Knee-high weeds grew from fissures in the pavement. There were scattered stacks and piles of threadbare tires and strips of black rubber throughout; rusted out mufflers, gas tanks, radiators and grills; engines that had long ago been stripped of anything useful.

Down, toward the right-hand part of the parking lot-cum-junkyard, where the dumpster was located and over-flowing to capacity with refuse, dead foliage, and an assortment of fractured and discarded bargain-basement, low-rent coffee tables and nightstands, sofas and chairs, toasters, crock pots, washers and dryers, refrigerators and other appliances, large and small, with additional mounds of plastic trash bags bloated and splitting at the seams, that surrounded it at the base, were a couple of stray dogs engaged in the act, something the boy had been exposed to enough times in the past, so that in and of itself held no real interest; only these two were caught up/entangled in such a way that he had never witnessed until now. Stuck, they were, ass-to-ass, literally; on all fours, heads at opposite ends. Evidently attempting to separate, to untangle, and not able to do so.

One would pull one way for a while, dragging the other with him, then the other mutt would pull, or try to, in his direction, forcing the other dog to back up, neither getting anywhere.

Mexican standoff? He couldn't say. All he knew was it was the Latino part of town. East LA. What was going on?

It was only moments earlier that they had been in front of the building. Fucking, to be sure, but doing it the way they were supposed to: the male, forepaws atop the other's hind end, while he pumped away from behind. The boy's mother, with whom the boy had walked up, having been thoroughly disgusted by the sight, had flung one of her pumps at them. The dogs hadn't bothered to separate—maybe even then had not been able to—instead had hopped the short distance to the left of the tenement to where the driveway and entrance to the lot in back was. And here they were, still at it, only coupled in this baffling manner.

What was it J.J., his dogcatcher step-daddy had said to him about it that time? Couldn't recall the exact words. "Ever see 'em stuck, boy, it's 'cause the bitch has got her snapper locked on the male's prick and he ain't gettin' out until he shoots his load in her. Then the head of his prick, fat like a light bulb, goes down; only then can the male take his dick back. Now, them young males don't get it; and it's fun to watch 'em panic, an' struggle to pull out. Ain't happening, no way. What a man who knows dogs does then is to calm the asshole down. Only thing that works. Calm the motherfucker down."

Cecil wondered if that's what was going on, if only in a casual way. Because the mongrels, the junkyard, and the heaps hardly mattered beyond what went on in them at night, as well as during the day: local prostitutes, some who lived in the building, sneaking about with their johns, junkies in a crazy frenzy to slam a needle somewhere, bums seeking out vehicles with missing seats to take a dump in.

He'd taken more than one girl to one of the forgotten sedans himself, gotten them to pull their panties down and show him what they had.

None of that rated this mid-morning. No. What mattered and preoccupied his thoughts were the spiders and fat flies he enjoyed burning to a crisp on his side of the window, the flies who threw themselves mindlessly against the pane, and the spiders lying in wait in various corners of the window frame and the traps they had spun for the purpose of snagging a meal.

The boy stood at the window, book of matches in hand, doing the thing that sent the familiar sensation through him: setting things on fire, living or not; fire did it for him. Even though it was beyond his comprehension how or why the mere sight of fire and destroying things in this fashion had the effect that it did on him, it did not stop him from yearning for more of the same.

Drawing his attention above his head, in a web in the upper right corner of the frame, a newly trapped fly struggled to untangle itself, to no avail. Spiders knew what they were doing. The web was sinewy, tough, and this spider's latest victim was not going anywhere.

As expected, the spider emerged soon enough from within its lair. Moved toward the prey. With bated breath, the kid waited until the predator was practically upon the doomed insect before striking the match, reaching up, and roasting them both.

There were other flies he pounced on, clutched in his fist, and dealt with. Large, glistening green flies, who made the loud buzzing, grating noise that added to the thrill, he caught and relieved them of their wings. They were incredibly easy to grab: dumb flies who kept throwing themselves against the grime-streaked glass as if they expected to be able to drill through somehow and escape out there to join up with thousands of their ilk at the dumpster below and anywhere else throughout the lot.

The boy snatched them up, yanked the wings off, and watched with something like inner satisfaction as they kicked out with their spindly legs on their backs, on the sill, kicking out frantically, that enhanced the experience for him. There was no denying it, no explaining it: the combo, fire and subsequent death, not only heightened the senses all around, but clearly left him in a state of arousal, just as there was no denying he felt responsible for what was taking place up there on the fourth floor.

Coco Garcia, the gap-toothed, obese Mexican woman who lived across the way from them in the other apartment and everyone knew to be a prostitute, who had, in fact, turned his mother on to some of her johns, poked her head out through her partially opened door.

"They're at it again, huh, kid? I wouldn't take that off no man. I hope she beats the shit out of his fag ass this time."

The boy said nothing. Looked up at her, then turned away to mind his spiders and flies. He was down to his remaining match and that bothered him. The big woman shook her head at the ongoing racket. She withdrew back into her place and closed her door.

"Lemme get this straight, bitch: You stayed out all night and a good part of the morning, and all you got to show for it is a handful of change? Why, you ain't even good at whorin'! To call you a whore would be an insult to all the hard-working whores out there! Hear what I'm saying, bitch? You ain't even good at whorin'! You don't rate!"

"It's the boy's birthday, Joe. I wanted to do something for the boy this once."

"You ain't even got enough coins left here for a bottle of *rotgut*—"

"He needed shoes, Joe. It's his birthday."

"How many times I gotta hear about the bastard's birthday, *goddamn you!* I ain't got enough here for a taste, and you got nerve to spend on shoes and birthday cakes and ice cream!"

"Can't you do without this one time? We'll get some money later—"

"Why should I have to do without, bitch? Why should I have to suffer? Didn't I tell you to abort the bastard? Didn't I?"

"There was no money for it, asshole! You drank everything I brought in—like you're doing now!"

"You're blaming me? *It's my fault?*"

There was a loud slap. The woman screamed. There was tumbling. Someone being thrown against a wall. More screaming and yelling. Mad dogs barked inside the apartment.

Eight-year-old Cecil Omar Biggs stood at the landing between the floors, struck the last match and burned a plump spider with it. Through with that, he was back on the green flies: easy to catch, while they kept at the filthy windowpane, buzzing away. He'd sever their wings and lower them on the window sill on their backs. Liked to watch them kick wildly this way.

He had an unusually large one now. Was desperate to burn it. Went through his pockets in search of matches. Dug up a book. No matches left in it. Kept searching, found another. A single match left. Struck it. Lowered the flame toward the frantic fly: the fat fucker. He wanted to kill them all. Nothing gave him more pleasure than killing these fuckers. And then he got him but good. The last match. That was it. Gone. All of them. What would he do? Keep catching them and tear their wings off. He'd have to find some more matches somewhere soon. While happening to look up toward the top of the windowpane at a couple of flies banging their heads against the glass, his eyes wandered up toward the ceiling, up there in both corners, large cobwebs, too, but he couldn't reach those. He wished that he could. There were also plenty of dead moths along the window sill that he felt like frying . . . but he needed matches for that.

The landing was littered: beer cans and soda bottles, cigarette butts and empty cartons, bologna packaging and candy bar wrappers, used condoms and Tampons. He shoved his worn sneaker around in there, in search of a possible match, a lighter . . . and found nothing. He cursed. Needed fire. The yelling and fighting in their apartment kept on: more things being broken; his father's dogs barked. Then he heard John Joseph release a deep howl. The apartment door opened like a cannon shot, and his mother, heavily made-up as usual, both eyes swollen, mouth bleeding, with all that wild dark hair flying and not a stitch of clothing on her, scrambled down the flight of stairs toward him.

There was panic and terror in her peepers; even, incredibly enough, to some degree, a kind of glee. He noticed, too, a couple of her front teeth were missing this time.

She descended the stairs in her clumsy, harried way, with John Joseph, drunk and slobbering, nose and jaw bloody, in his soiled OD green army boxers and worn, mis-matched white socks, staggering in the doorway, the birthday cake haphazardly balanced on the palm of his left hand, while he held onto the doorjamb with the other to steady his aim. He cursed and hurled the cake at her, the birthday cake that she'd only bought moments earlier. J.J. sent the cake flying through the air as she neared the landing where the boy stood. The youngster turned his back in time. The cake grazed the top of her head, and a good deal of it deflected and spattered the back of the boy's neck.

"Half a whore!"

"Up yours, faggot!"

The boy's mother continued on down the next flight to make her way toward the lobby below.

"I'll kill you, bitch! Kill the both of you!"

John Joseph ducked back inside, to reappear seconds later with the box the boy's new footwear was in and pitched the shoes, one at a time, at the eight-year-old.

One shoe bounced off the top of the boy's head and went sailing through the windowpane, causing him to pivot enough for the second shoe to nail him between the eyes. The blow sent the kid spinning into the corner, his face buried in his hands. He wasn't crying, merely doing his best to deal with the throbbing pain.

ZOOK

By KIRK ALEX

Blurb & Novel Excerpt

Some very strange things are taking place at the New Pueblo Funeral Home . . .

War vet, Ray Zook, a PTSD afflicted former grunt, is about to regret that he ever set foot in Tucson, Arizona.

All he wants is to gain the courage to face his inner-demons and somehow explain to the widow of his best friend what *really* happened to him during their stint in the military. But when Zook is mugged and takes a temporary job working the night-shift at a crematory run by a couple of unsavory employees, those plans get derailed.

After witnessing a series of disturbing incidents—like the shady "after hours" business taking place—that hurl him into an immoral world of grave robbing, coffin swapping, and even disappearing bodies, Zook finds himself caught in the middle of a twisted power-struggle to control ownership of the funeral home.

If Zook hopes to escape this utter mess with his sanity intact, he must rise above his fears and confront the dark deeds before he ends up back in the looney bin . . . for good this time.

Chapter 1

I had just gotten off the bus and the two of them followed me: the dim-witted young chick with the dishwater hair and the beastly two-hundred-pound butch dyke with her: all tats and rings and studs and chains. Lots of black leather. Blue/black crew cut. Demanding money.

"For what?"

"BJ."

The other one was quiet. Just wasn't there mentally. Didn't seem like it mattered to her, either. It was the bitch built like a dozer who was after my cash. I dared her to take it, which hadn't been a wise move at all. She cold-cocked me. By the time she was done I was on the ground, nearly out. She'd flipped me over on my belly and sat on my back. I could hardly breathe, let alone do much of anything else at this point. She'd taken my wallet, extracted the bills, tossed it back at me. Spit in my direction, and they walked off. With close to eighty dollars of my jack. My roll. A good chunk of it. If it hadn't been for the paper money I'd kept stashed inside my sock I'd have been up the creek. I was, but at least with what remained I'd be able to rent a room, buy something to eat, a newspaper, and look for work.

I had been sound asleep, as comfortable as one can possibly be on a Greyhound bus. Been pulling on a bottle of hooch all the way from Phoenix. The idea was to stay on in Tucson long enough to beef up the roll and continue on to Ft. Worth. The ex had family there and I hoped that's where she'd ended up. I didn't have a need to connect with her. It came down to my kid. In her early teens by now. Hadn't seen her in years. I'd been to LaFayette, Indiana; Bowling Green, Kentucky; Lawrence, Kansas, and dozens of other towns, large and small. I stayed on the move; perpetual motion seemed to keep the demons at bay—at least I had myself convinced of it. I had war-related nightmares I couldn't shake, and some other things I was trying to live down. Staying on the move seemed to be the answer. Only how in hell do you get away from yourself? I'd been given the boot by more apartment managers and motel desk clerks for kicking the floor and walls in my sleep than I cared to remember.

It was usually some indiscriminate setting, me unarmed, being chased by the enemy in some far-off land. Commies? Mid-East zealots? Your run-of-the-mill America haters? Who knew? Or maybe I was in denial. Unwilling to face my demons. It took a lot to deal with that shit.

That was where they got on, though: Phoenix. The young one: couldn't tell how old, didn't look half bad in tight jeans, pink blouse, although the heavy one with the butch cut made me want to retch. This was one unappealing broad. And wouldn't you know it, she was the one who dropped her sweaty and mean ass in the seat next to mine. She wanted a hit off my hooch. I told her to piss off. Took the occasional nip from the bottle, pulled the blanket up to about my neck. I had no idea how long I'd be staying in Tucson. Didn't know a soul in town, not really. It was just a place to drive through, or maybe spend a week in, look around. Been in the 'Old Pueblo' before. Worked as a busser at some sports bar some years back, did a bit of panhandling.

What nudged me awake was the two of them switching seats. Now the young one was sitting next to me. Before the fat one gave up her seat, she whispered in my ear: "My cousin gives great head."

"How much?"

"Forty bucks."

I told her to get lost.

They switched seats, and before I knew it, 'cousin' had her hand under my blanket. Inched it slowly toward my crotch and was rubbing it, just running her fingers gently over it, and I'll be damned if my groin didn't begin to stir. All that vino, and there I was: getting wood. She proceeded to unzip my fly. I let her; pretended I was asleep, and let her do what she wanted. I figured if I acted like I was dozing, they wouldn't be able to claim I owed them money later, her and the beast she was with.

She had it out, stroking, slowly, taking her time. Then she ducked her head under the blanket. I let her. Of course, I let her. It had been a while. No love, no sex. Traveling the country on buses, when the money was there, hitching when it wasn't.

She had her tongue on it, licking; then she had the shaft inside, all of it. I didn't have a tremendous whole lot, but it was all right; there were some poor bastards who envied what I did have. You lived with the hand the Dealer laid on you—and this time the Dealer had shown me some kindness, I thought. That head of hers bobbed up and down, not fast, gently, gradually, taking her time. And the fact that it was night provided adequate cover. Passengers were zoned out, with the exception of some punk in his teens, across the aisle, watching out of the corner of his eye. Let him. Probably wished he was me, the big shot, getting his nuts off on a Greyhound bus to nowhere.

The licking went on. She played with the head, flicking it thoroughly. This chick had been around, knew her business when it came to licking balls and sucking cock. It had been such a long time, too. Probably did this to get by: sucked off strangers for whatever they could pick up. Who knew? Did it matter? Only I'd had too much wine. Couldn't make it. It was no good. Wine and sex didn't mix, not for me.

She lifted her head. I pulled out my wallet. Extracted a tenner for her effort. She did what she could. Not her fault. Before the young hooker had had a chance to even take a good look at it, the beast, her freakish 'relation,' stuck her hand in and snapped up the sawbuck. She sniffed it. Looked it over. She was not pleased. Tough, I thought. That was a ten-dollar try.

"My name is not Bill Gates and I don't own *Microsoft*. Besides, I never got off."

"You're lying." She yanked her 'cousin' out of the seat, and lowered that wide posterior next to me.

"We agreed on forty."

"Like hell we did."

"That was a forty-dollar BJ. You never had anything that good in your life."

"How would you know? Maybe I had better." For a fact. Only my ex-wives wanted nothing to do with me, especially the last one. I had no idea where she was. Ft. Worth was nothing more than a guess, a vague one, like all the other towns I'd been to. She'd taken the kid and disappeared off the face of the earth. Could explain the roaming. If I admitted it to myself. I didn't need the exes back, only ached to see the kid. A girl. Must have been six years ago I saw her last. I didn't blame the wife for leaving me. Couldn't take the screaming in the middle of the night, the kicking at the floor with my feet, the times I was stationed out of the country, or stuck in some bug bin here in the states. I drank to fight the demons. Only made everything worse. They had me on *Prozak*, then *Paxil*, at the VA. While I was in the whack ward the wife dropped the bomb: wanted out. I couldn't stop her, didn't try. She never mentioned custody, only because she figured she was entitled. She'd given birth to the child and that was that. Frankly, I was in no shape to take care of a kid, couldn't even take care of myself. I let it go; let them both go. The ex had a man, in fact, had been shagging a neighbor while I was stationed overseas. The way it usually went. I'd had it done to me once before. Kid could be his, biologically. Probably. Don't matter. I treated her like she was my own. You get emotionally attached. Kids are all right. Always wanted a family. Always did. Things kept going wrong somehow. Something would always happen to turn things upside down. This was divorce number three. You know what they say: three strikes and you're out. Three marriages, three divorces. I was defective, a loser. Something was seriously the matter with me. It was the war; it was other things.

"I doubt it." She looked at me. "Not with that nose and those teeth." My nose was bent, both ways, in bar brawls that I usually started and lost, so were my teeth—born with them that way—the ones still there: black, yellow. Of the uppers in front, I had but one left. In the middle.

I pulled the blanket up, and pretended to go to sleep. Only she wouldn't let me.

"Thirty bucks. You can't deny that was worth thirty bucks."

"You got what it was worth. And that's the end of it. I never got rocks. You bitches came on to me. Before I knew what was going on, your nympho girlfriend was molesting my privates."

"You owe us money."

"Fuck off, or I go to the driver."

"He's our friend. That wouldn't get you anywhere."

"What does *he* pay for it?"

"That's a different case. He gets a discount—and has nothing to do with you."

"I feel drained for some strange reason and crave rest." And this time I shut my eyes and kept them shut. I could feel them switch seats again. As she got up, I turned my head, and caught her cousin going down on some geezer way in the back. I guessed the freak was on her feet in order to collect payment, and before I knew it, the young bitch was back sitting beside me. It wasn't long before she had her hand under my blanket again. This time I slapped it away, and she left me alone.

We got off the bus. I had my old backpack; walking down in search of a cheap motel along Drachman. Then I turned down an alley. Big mistake. They'd had friends waiting for them. Indians. Looked like. I was jumped, knocked down. She stood on one side, while one of those drunk Indian friends of hers stood on the other, and they took turns delivering a couple of very effective, if unsteady, kicks to my kidneys. The beast had emptied my wallet, rummaged through the backpack, spat in disgust and left me lying there in the puke and blood.

Welcome to Tucson, Arizona. To be fair, this was no slam against the Old Pueblo, and besides, the bitches had hopped on in Phoenix.

I was up, wiped vomit from my chin. Dug my hand inside my left sock. At least I still had that. Jammed the spare socks and underwear, photo album, toiletries, back in the pack. Checked into a motel, washed my face, showered, then plopped down on the floor and slept the rest of the night and most of the next day when I had to go out and find a bar, or *Circle K*, to buy a can of *Spam* and a 6- Pack of *Red Dog*, a newspaper. At this rate, my money wouldn't last long and I'd be stuck here indefinitely. Taking a look at the job ads was in order.

* * *

ZIGGY POPPER AT LARGE

14 TALES OF GENERAL DEGENERACY, OF MAYHEM & DEBAUCHERY – FOR THE MORALLY CONFLICTED & BORDERLINE CRIMINAL

– Not For Prudes Or The Easily Offended –

Raw & real, filthy & funny gutbucket dispatches from the gritty streets of LA by Kirk Alex, author of the acclaimed & controversial **LUSTMORD: Anatomy of a Serial Butcher . . .**

It's a hot mother of an afternoon in seedy East Hollywood. Ziggy Popper is fresh out of the joint, sitting in a dive bar nursing a beer and minding his own business, when a scrawny loser walks in & parks his skinny butt on the stool next to his . . . and offers him cash money to shag his shack job. Even shows him a faded still of a wench tied down to a bed, spread eagle, with nothing on but a blindfold. The bitch of it is the female in the photo resembles Ziggy's ex a great deal, the one who helped send him to prison.

It's more than enough to make Ziggy want to take this on. From there, Kirk Alex's story takes a wild and unpredictable turn. Hardboiled and packing a punch of LA attitude in its gritty realism and black humor, "Ziggy Popper" shows what can happen when a man's past catches up to him. Even in the middle of a steamy sex scene.

About the Author

Kirk Alex's novel *Lustmord: Anatomy of a Serial Butcher* was a finalist in the Kindle Book Review's Best Book Awards of 2014. He is also the author of *Zook, Fifty Shades of Tinsel*, the story collection: *Ziggy Popper at Large,* the *Love, Lust & Murder* series*: Throwback & Backlash*, the Eddie "Doc" Holiday Private Eye Series, and a few other novels & shorts.

IF YOU ENJOYED THIS BOOK . . .

Dear Reader, if you enjoyed this book, won't you please consider posting a review wherever you deem suitable. Thank you kindly.